THE MURDERER'S SON

It began with the savage murder of a young man in the Surrey town of Woking. Months later, private investigator Frank Crane is sent to the town on a missing persons case, hired by a woman called Jane Kennedy. But why is his car being followed? Crane realizes that Jane is at risk, but who is out to get her? Why are the police involved and two DCs brutally beaten? Crane uncovers the appalling truth, and soon he and Jane are on the run from a depraved killer . . .

Books by Richard Haley
Published by The House of Ulverscroft:

WRITTEN IN WATER

RICHARD HALEY

◆

THE MURDERER'S SON

Complete and Unabridged

ULVERSCROFT
Leicester

First published in Great Britain in 2006 by
Robert Hale Limited
London

First Large Print Edition
published 2007
by arrangement with
Robert Hale Limited
London

British Library CIP Data

Haley, Richard
    The murderer's son.—Large print ed.—
Ulverscroft large print series: crime
1. Missing persons—Fiction 2. Private investigators
—Fiction 3. Suspense fiction 4. Large type books
I. Title
823.9′14 [F]

ISBN 978–1–84617–781–1

Published by
F. A. Thorpe (Publishing)
Anstey, Leicestershire
Set by Words & Graphics Ltd.
Anstey, Leicestershire
Printed and bound in Great Britain by
T. J. International Ltd., Padstow, Cornwall

This book is printed on acid-free paper

1

She heard raised voices then. She went to the window. Tony stood head and shoulders above the other. He was stooping slightly, speaking into the stocky man's face. He only did that when he was very angry. She knew. But the short man was angry too. His face was red and there was a wild gleam in his pale eyes and he was shaking. Then Tony shouted at him, and she actually heard those words through the double-glazing. 'Oh God,' she almost sobbed, 'anything but that. *Anything*!' She scrabbled with the window-handle. She had to stop them. Both men's hands were bunching into fists. But the window-locks were still on. She snatched a key from a chest of drawers, got it into the lock with a shaking hand, glanced down again at the angry men. Something suddenly flashed in the stocky man's hand. Her insides seemed to fill with iced water. It couldn't be a knife, it couldn't be. It was just a silly argument for Christ's sake! But it was a knife. Tony's face had turned white. He struck out at the man. If his big fist had connected he'd have knocked him halfway across the road.

But the man dodged the blow, almost contemptuously, and while Tony was still wrong-footed from the blow that hadn't connected, plunged the knife into his chest. His eyes widened in shock. She'd never seen anyone in such a state of shock. He simply couldn't believe it. He suddenly struck out again, with both hands, a flurry of blows. The small man dodged every one, then stabbed Tony again in the chest. Blood was spurting across Tony's white T-shirt. He looked dazed, lost, incredulous. He was weakening; in seconds. He tried to throw his arms around the man as if to pin him down, but he was always too fast. Red-faced, mad-eyed, lips glistening with saliva, he stabbed Tony a third time, a fourth. The bloodstained knife was almost a blur now in a hand that moved like a piston. Tony's T-shirt was more bloodstained than white, the stains wet and dripping. The woman felt as if the breath had been knocked out of her. Her heart felt to be pressing against her lungs. She couldn't get a sound out. She closed her eyes. It couldn't be happening, could it? It *couldn't* be happening. When she opened her eyes it would be to see Tony bringing round their old Astra. But when she did open them, Tony lay crumpled on the tarmac, his eyes glazing, blood dripping into a pool. The stocky man turned away, glancing up as if sensing her presence. Their eyes met in a long look. In hers, numb, near-catatonic shock, in his, a look of satisfaction.

A car-horn sounded; briefly, as if it had been given the lightest touch. The small man put the red-bladed knife carefully away, then loped off diagonally to where the car was parked. The car was rolling even as he closed the door. She was in too stunned a state to note the number. Not that it mattered. She knew who the small man was. Who didn't round here?

★   ★   ★

Benson rang the door-bell of the small detached. It took so long for the door to be opened he'd almost moved on. Before it was answered he counted three locks being released. The door was also kept on the chain when a woman opened it. She looked to be mid-twenties, middle height, curvy, long brown hair. She also looked frightened.

'I'm police, madam,' he told her. 'Detective Sergeant Benson.' He held up his warrant card. 'Could you spare me a moment of your time?'

She watched him in silence for a few

3

seconds. 'You're . . . not one of the usual ones . . . '

'Usual ones?' He gave her a puzzled glance.

She closed her full lips in a firm straight line. Her eyes looked guarded now. She closed the door slightly to draw the chain, then opened it wider. 'Do you want to come in?'

He stepped into the hallway. 'This won't take long. Did you know that an expensive motor had been stolen from the house at the top end of the cul-de-sac?'

She raised her eyebrows slightly, shook her head.

'Mercedes. Top of the range. Brand new. It was in a locked garage and had an immobilizer. But someone managed to steal it.'

'Oh.' She gave him a blank look.

'There's a gang,' he told her. 'They only steal expensive new cars. They take them abroad, sell them at a discount, no questions asked. That much we do know. Well, we're just asking around. I don't suppose you saw anyone acting suspiciously two nights ago? Didn't look out of your bedroom window lateish on and notice or hear anything?'

'I'm . . . afraid not. Nothing at all.'

He sighed. 'It would be a long shot if you had. But sometimes someone *does* see something that helps. I'll not take up more of your time.'

He turned to go. She suddenly said, 'Can you help me with a missing person?'

He gave her a sharp glance. She seemed a bit odd. First saying he wasn't one of the usual ones and now thinking he got involved with mis-pers.

'You'd really need to go to the station in town for that,' he said, trying to conceal his indifference and anxious now to move on. Christ, they had two cars a week disappearing and he'd had yet another bollocking about it this morning.

'I keep ringing and ringing but she never answers,' she said sadly. 'And she's always there normally. Especially since . . . ' She broke off.

Benson glanced at his watch, reminding himself that he had a duty to be courteous to the public at all times. 'Why not go and call on her?'

'She lives in Surrey.'

Benson was beginning to wonder what the woman was all about. 'Call in at the station and give them all the details. But I think they'll tell you that if your friend really is missing it would be a job for the police on the spot.'

'I don't really want to trouble the police.

Any police.' Was that a note of alarm he heard in her voice? 'Do you know of anyone else who could help? A private man . . . investigator?'

'Yes,' he said. 'There's a man called Crane. Frank Crane. He might be able to help . . . '

★   ★   ★

He saw Crane at the Toll Gate.

'Some woman called Jane Kennedy might be ringing you. I gave her your name. Some kind of a mis-per. Sort of odd though.'

'How odd?' Crane said warily.

'She has a friend who lives in Surrey. Very close. Phone never answered in two weeks. Jane Kennedy's anxious to know where she is. Doesn't want to involve the police.'

'Why not?'

'Wouldn't say. Maybe she wanted some quick answers. It's the set-up that seems a bit odd. Nice-looking kid who seems to be on her own. I was just doing a routine door-to-door about the fancy wheels being nicked. Took her the best part of a minute to undo all the door-locks.'

'Thanks for bearing me in mind, Ted.'

Crane didn't think he'd spoken in a pointed way, but the other reddened as if he had. Benson finished his half of bitter, glanced at his glass, then at his watch, and said, 'Well, I need to get moving. I'll see you around.'

Crane watched him go. He couldn't wait to get away these days. At one time they'd come in here most evenings around six and have two drinks each, to keep below the limit. Benson would buy one round, Crane the other. They'd talk over the day, joke around, have a laugh. But things had been different then. He sighed, signalled for Dave to pour his second drink.

★　★　★

She rang Crane later. 'It's about a missing person,' she said.

'DS Benson mentioned it. I know him personally. I'm not sure I can help you.'

'I don't mind what it costs.'

It would have given Crane a warm glow to have heard that when he was just starting out. These days, with a full book, he could afford to be very choosy.

'Why not report it to the local police down in Surrey?'

'Do you think it would do much good?' she said, in a low voice.

It was a fair point. The police bracketed missing persons with back-burners unless a kid was involved. 'The woman has no friends or relations you can contact?'

'No. And I can't go myself.'

'Why is that?'

'Please come and see me. I'll explain it all then.'

'I'm very busy right now. It would take me a day to drive to Surrey and back and do what I'd need to do.'

'I'll pay. I know it won't be cheap.'

'That's not the point. Let's say I could use the time more productively.'

'But I'd pay you enough to make up for that.'

She wasn't for giving in, in that small sad voice of hers. Crane thought for a few seconds. 'All right. I'll call this evening, yes? Six-thirty. Have all the facts ready and I'll consider it. But I can't promise anything.'

He cleared his mobile, looked out through the rain-spattered windscreen of his station-ary car at the wet, glistening, city road. He still didn't think he wanted to know. But she'd sounded so desperate. He had to accept that he was intrigued. A woman apparently alone behind a bunch of door-locks, not wanting to go to Surrey herself, not wanting even to contact the police. He gave a wry smile, turned the key in the ignition. It would be a stupid, banal affair, they nearly always

8

were in the end. He knew if anyone did. But sometimes the illusion of what might be an interesting case gave a little edge to the tedium of his days. And it wouldn't cost him anything.

★   ★   ★

She stood at the front window a little before half past six. It overlooked a small garden that was mainly lawn. There were a few roses in the borders, a few carnations, some gaudy lavatera. It was badly tended and everything straggled. A man came maybe once a fortnight to cut the grass. He was supposed to weed but hardly ever did. She was indifferent to the way it looked, hardly even saw it. What was it to her?

It was raining, vertically and hard, as it had rained on and off most of the afternoon. It made the Blackbird Common estate look as if no one lived there. But it looked like that a lot of the time anyway, whether it rained or not. It was obviously one of the reasons why she . . .

A car emerged slowly through the near-tropical down-pour, rain bouncing off the roof in a haze of moisture. He would be checking the house numbers. He braked in front of hers. She felt queasy. Had she got her story right? She'd gone over it time and again. Would he buy it? He didn't sound like a man who bought much. She shouldn't have done it. She knew the risks involved. If this Frank Crane turned it down she'd maybe have to let it go. There'd be other investigators, but Crane came recommended, and he didn't need the work, so he had to be good. She had to find Dora. 'Oh, Dora,' she murmured, 'I do miss you.'

Crane got out of the car, opened an umbrella, walked rapidly up the drive. He expected to hear the door-locks being undone, but that wasn't the case this evening. Maybe she'd undone them in advance because she was expecting him. She kept the chain on even so, watching him guardedly through the four-inch gap.

'Frank Crane. I can show you my photo-card driving licence if you need verification.'

She shook her head. 'No, it's all right. Come in, please.'

She led him along the hallway and into what looked to be part dining-room, part living. She motioned silently to an armchair and she took another one. The furniture had a job-lot look to it. Crane wondered if the house was a furnished rental. On Blackbird Common there were quite a few buy-to-lets.

One small section of a gas-fire hissed thinly.

'Thanks for agreeing to see me, Mr Crane.'

'Frank.'

'I'm Jane, then. Tea, coffee?'

'Just talk to me, Jane.'

She really did look very sad. But he met a lot of sad people in his line of work. And she lived alone with a lot of door-locks on, so maybe she had a lot to be sad about. There'd be a bloke in it somewhere. There usually was.

'I suppose you'll think this very strange.'

'Try me.'

She leaned forward a little, hands clasped. She had a broad face, very pale, with a bulbous nose, full lips, square regular teeth. She had a slight cast in one of her amber eyes. Slight casts did nothing for nine women in ten. She was the tenth and it did a great deal. Good shape too, but she was over-weight. And there was something odd about her hair. It was chestnut, long, wavy, but had barely detectable blonde roots. That was a first for Crane, a natural blonde keen to be a brunette. He took in all this on auto-pilot in the few seconds before she spoke again.

'Do you know Woking?'

'No. I suppose it's in Surrey.'

'It's all motorway from here. Turn-off eleven on the M25 westbound.'

'Let's not get ahead of ourselves here. *If* I went to Woking why would I be going?'

She glanced uneasily through the patio door. The rain was so heavy the glass of the door was covered in an unbroken sheet of running water. The shadows of the gloomy day seemed to underline what made her so unhappy. Crane had learnt long ago never to get involved in clients' emotional states, but few clients came in such a state of obvious distress.

'My friend, Dora Powell lives on Eastern Lane. It's quite central. I'd like you to see if she's . . . if she's all right . . . '

'Keep talking.'

Her heavy eyes rested on his for several more silent seconds. 'She's my closest friend. We had a dreadful falling out. I hurt her very badly.' She clasped her hands again. 'About . . . about a month ago I gave her a ring. Asked her to forgive me. Pleaded. We . . . well, at least we talked a bit. It was very difficult. I went on ringing her and she'd always talk a little. Not for very long and . . . and she'd never ring me. But I *know* she wants it to be the way it was, as much as I do. The old close friendship. But I upset her so badly . . . '

Her hesitant, husky voice trailed off.

'What was it about, the upset?'

Her eyes met his again, shifted away. Not a good sign to a man who did signs. 'That's the trouble, it was so trivial to begin with. I don't know how it got out of hand. It was just a silly woman's thing, but we both said too many hurtful things we didn't mean.'

They sat in another brief silence, broken only by the hissing of the fire and the endless patter of rain on the windows. Crane leaned back, irritation beginning to set in. This told him nothing. He was about to say so, in different words, when she went on.

'These past two weeks, whenever I've rung, she's simply not been there.'

'Maybe she's not answering the phone.'

'If she was there she'd answer.' She smiled faintly for the first time. It did a lot for her, like the cast. 'She's a woman. Have you ever known a woman who'd ignore a ringing phone?'

It was a good point. 'This Dora Powell, she lives alone?'

'She does now. She's married, but they split. She kept the house.' She was speaking more carefully now. Another bad sign for Crane. If she was watching her words she could be giving him a version of the truth, and if he was only getting a version he didn't want the work.

'Maybe she's taken a holiday.'

13

'She told me she'd nothing planned before the autumn. They always went late, she and Harry, when they were together, to avoid the school holidays.'

There was a touch of colour then in each of her pale cheeks.

'Maybe she and Harry got it back together again. Second honeymoon.'

She shook her head firmly. 'No, he won't be back.'

'You seem very sure.'

'I know. Believe me, I know.'

Crane felt he might be homing in on the real story at last. 'Jane,' he said evenly, 'Harry going and Dora being very angry wouldn't be anything to do with *you* and Harry, would it?'

Her mouth fell open in what looked to be total surprise. There was even a spark of animation in her eyes, another first. 'Oh, *no*. It was nothing like that. How could it be? If you understood the situation — '

She broke off abruptly.

'That's what I'm trying to do, get my head round it.'

'I mean . . . ' she said, almost forcing out the words, 'I mean I used to work in Woking. I met Dora through my job. I'd not been born there, hadn't many friends. Dora was like a . . . like an older sister to me. Took me under her wing, you know? I'd go to her place for meals, stay nights . . . ' Her voice thickened with emotion and for a couple of seconds she couldn't go on. She shook her head slightly, pushed herself on in a stronger tone. 'But Harry, he was a nice man, always pleasant and friendly, but there was nothing between us. Truly. You must believe me.'

He did. Because maybe the love interest had not been Harry but Dora herself. She was the one the kid seemed to be getting upset about. Would she have filled up like that had it just been a routine friendship, however close? And maybe Harry had cleared off because Dora had become keener on a bit of how's your sister than him. He wasn't going to go into that. As far as he was concerned it was off limits, added nothing to the case, and she'd deny it anyway. 'Look,' he said, 'so you don't think the police would give it much attention. I'm inclined to agree. But there must be *someone* down there you could contact who knows Dora.'

She shook her head. 'No one. My only contacts were Dora and Harry and — ' She broke off yet again. He heard the sound of indrawn breath.

'And?'

She looked at him vaguely. She looked to have lost the thread of what she was saying. 'I . . . I was going to say I'd no idea where

Harry was living, so I couldn't contact him even.'

So why had she broken off without saying that?

'Look, Jane, why not just go down there yourself?'

'Oh, I can't,' she said quickly. 'Not right now. I work for a small team of financial advisers. Carr Lane. One of the refurbished warehouses. There are a lot of new products on the boil, we're all working flat out, bringing work home at the weekends. We'll not be on top for at least a month. It's a hassle but the money's good. It's . . . it's why I came north.'

He could believe most of that. She was wearing a long straight skirt in charcoal bouclé and a grey knitted top. There'd probably be a long-line jacket to complete the ensemble. It would make her look very competent around an office. The dark colours were a good match for the intense sadness; the brown hair too that masked a natural blondeness when other women spent hundreds of pounds colouring brown hair blonde.

'To Bradford?' he said, with a wry grin. 'What did London do wrong, or Manchester or Leeds?'

'The opening was here. The firm's making

plans to move to Leeds in a few months. I didn't fancy the cattle-truck commute to London, and it was too expensive to live there.'

'Still, a long way from Woking. This was *after* the bust-up with your friend?'

She gave a slight nod. The indrawn breath was there again. A woman he'd once known had told him the pain was exactly the same whether it was a man or a woman you were off your head about. And she'd been in a position to know. He sat back and thought for a few seconds. Now he'd got it together most of it seemed to add up. But did he want the work? There was an almost pleading look in those heavy, grieving eyes. He rubbed a cheek. It would take only a day. It would make a break from the routine slog. And despite himself, he felt sorry for the kid.

'Please help me . . . Frank.' She seemed to have a direct line to his brain.

'All right.' He took out his notebook. 'Give me your friend's address. And we're talking turn-off eleven on the Heathrow side of the M25 . . . '

'Thank you, Frank, thank you so much. Take the A320 from junction eleven. It takes you directly to Woking. It's only a few miles. There's a canal that runs through the centre. It has a big car-park at the side of it. You can't miss it. Best to park there; parking anywhere else can be difficult. Cross the main road, walk up through the shopping centre and you'll come to the railway station. Take the underpass and Eastern Lane's a little beyond. Number fifty-seven. Do you need any money upfront?'

He shook his head. 'I'll bill you later.'

'Whatever your bottom line comes to, add on fifty per cent. It'll be worth it to me.'

He could believe it. 'Well, we'll see . . . '

'I mean it, Frank.'

'Does Dora work?'

'Not since — ' She broke off, turned away slightly. 'Not since Harry made enough for her not to. He still gives her a good allowance.'

'So when she's not shopping and so on she's normally about the house?'

She nodded. 'But she's not there. I know it. I've tried at different times of the day.'

'I'll trace her, don't worry.'

'I don't want anyone to know I'm involved. It's important. Very important.' There was a sudden urgent note in her husky voice.

'Not even if I find Dora herself?'

'No. If you can find out where she is just let me know and I'll take it from there.'

He nodded. He'd taken the job, so she now called the tune.

'Describe Dora for me. A photo would help.'

'I've no photo.' He could tell from her tone she only wished she had. 'She's late forties, about my height. Dark hair, blue-grey eyes and a nose that tilts up a little. I believe there's a word for it.'

'*Retroussé?*'

She nodded. Late forties made her older than the number Crane had allotted her. She said she'd seen Dora as an older sister, but there weren't too many sisters born with a twenty-five-year age gap. Why not mother figure? Maybe that would have jarred with the relationship he'd guessed had developed. He put away his notebook. 'And she lives completely alone? No sons or daughters looking in?'

She had a big problem answering this. Her eyes slid from his to gaze in that odd, vacant way at the dripping trees and bushes of the back garden. She swallowed. Several times. 'They're . . . she's childless,' she said eventually. 'She's quite alone now.'

'You'll want the work doing as quickly as possible,' he said, with a faint sigh. It wasn't just Jane Kennedy, they all did.

'Please. I know you're a busy man.'

'Well, I can't do it tomorrow, but I think I can arrange things so I can go the day after.'

'I can't begin to thank you,' she said, in a low voice.

'I'll find her, Jane.'

'I know you will. I knew right away.'

Well, that was nice. His wasn't a line where you got too many pats on the back. Aggravation more like, when people thought you could work for ten pounds an hour, expenses included. That was why he always spelt out his charges very, very carefully. Except that this well-paid city girl didn't want to know.

They got up. She was about five-eight. She really did have a nice figure, but she needed to watch the weight gain. There was a lot of it about these days. What were the statistics, one in four and getting worse? But he'd read that some people over-ate when they were unhappy, some kind of a comfort thing. And she was certainly pining. For Dora? Crane took out his notebook again.

'Look,' he said, 'maybe I'd better have your office number just in case I need to contact you during the day.'

'No,' she said quickly, 'sorry. The partners have an absolute rule: no private calls on office phones. We get too much traffic. Just this number. I'm always here after six.'

Her amber eyes had widened. They showed something more than sadness this time. It could almost have been fear. He shrugged. 'All right.' He didn't ask for her mobile number, he knew she'd not want to answer that either in that pressure-cooker of an office. 'I'll ring you here when I get back from Woking. It may not be good news, but at least you'll know where you stand. I hope it will be good news.'

She nodded wanly, gave him what looked to be a stoic smile. He guessed she was going to have a lot to be stoic about if anything *had* happened to Dora on top of that almighty bust-up they'd had. It didn't seem fair. He found himself wishing she could be like the others then, of her age, who giggled in the pub over a drink, and were mad about some bloke or other, and stilted along Arndale Mall with a mobile glued to their ear.

The second he was through the front door it closed behind him. He heard the bolts and deadlocks clunking into place. It sounded like prison doors you heard being locked in films. Maybe the house began to feel a bit like a prison to sad Jane Kennedy when she'd turned the key on all that hardware.

It was a thought that came back later. Many times.

He crossed to his Megane through the ceaseless down-pour, the rain drumming on his old umbrella, and got in. He glanced round at the other houses as he cleared the windscreen. Blackbird Common was a newish development: bungalows, standard detacheds and small blocks of flats. It had well-tended verges and ornamental trees, but it had never been an area estate agents described as 'sought after', especially for family accommodation. It was on the north-eastern fringes of the city and inconvenient for schools. Retired people lived mainly in the bungalows, professional couples in the bigger houses, singletons in the flats. There were a few families in the four-beds, who had cars and the time to ferry kids around. It made for a very quiet estate. Not the sort of place that made you think of barbecues and communal activities. Crane wondered why she'd taken a house there. It just seemed to intensify her isolation. Her place was to the right of a large oblong, like a hammerhead, which formed a cul-de-sac to the straight road that led into it. The houses opposite and flanking hers had a remote and faceless look. Estates didn't come much handier if you were keen to keep yourself to yourself. Which is what she seemed to want.

★ ★ ★

She watched him going along the drive through the tiny viewing-glass set in the front door, a tall broad man in a grey flannel suit. Not much in the way of looks, rather coarse fair hair and plain features, but a lot of presence. She liked it, that blunt manner he had. And his smile, which didn't come often, was a nice warm one that took the edge off the clipped tones. She knew he'd find Dora, wherever she was. Oh, Dora . . .

She watched him shake out the umbrella and get in his car. Gave a sigh of relief. He had bought the story, after all. It had been a near thing. You couldn't get much past him with that sharp mind of his. But he'd accepted her reasons for not wanting to involve the police, for not being able to go to Woking herself right now, even though she could see he'd thought it odd. She smiled her faint forlorn smile. But she'd been lucky. He'd decided that she and Dora must be lesbians. She could tell. And he probably thought Harry had left Dora because of that.

She watched Crane looking about him. He had to be wondering why she lived in such a God-awful dump, obviously on her own. If only he knew. But he was a pro and he accepted it was nothing to do with him. She wished she could tell him the real truth. That she really did love Dora, loved her very much, but not in the way Crane thought. And that she had to know where she was, and how she was, and if they'd ever be able to meet up again one day. They'd shared so much. It had made things just a little easier; when they could talk now and then of the times before; when they'd met at the building society and got on so well. Soon it had been going to lunch and doing their shopping together, and then it had been going to Dora and Harry's place for meals, and then staying over on Saturday nights, and then . . .

When she came to, the bedside clock glowed on the figures 2.37. She was lying on top of the bed, fully dressed. The damp chill that had followed the rain must have woken her. She'd no idea how she'd got there. She would have been thinking about the old times again. She sat up on the bed. She knew it was that. They'd talked to her, spent a lot of time with her, but she still hadn't learnt how to handle it. How many of these black-out things had she had now? She was so scared. Not just endlessly lonely, but very, very scared.

★ ★ ★

'I need to go to Woking tomorrow, Maggie. Surrey. Rejig will you.'

'It won't be easy. Roper's were hoping you'd get your arse along there tomorrow. They know who it is this time, but they don't know how he's doing it.'

'Tell them I'll be there first thing Friday.' He gave her brief details of Jane Kennedy's search for Dora Powell.

'I'd say Roper's came ahead of a mis-per, if you want my opinion.'

'I don't, particularly.'

'Did you get anything on account?'

'No, she checks out.'

Maggie sniffed. She thought mis-pers were a total waste of time, unless they were legatees to substantial wills.

Crane said, 'Let me run this past you. Why should a woman with the sort of wavy blonde hair to kill for want to colour it brown?'

She sat back from the post she was opening. 'Blondes stand out in a crowd.'

'And Blackbird Common's a very remote place to lose yourself in.'

'Maybe she's on the run. Abusive boy-friend, money problems, maybe even worse,' she said dourly.

'Maybe. Nothing that concerns me. I'm just curious.'

'It sounds funny. You want to be careful. I seem to remember a similar affair.'

She rarely let him forget. He'd once been badly fooled, but the woman had had remarkable acting skills. You couldn't act the kind of bottomless sadness he'd seen in Jane Kennedy's eyes.

2

He was on the motorway by seven, east on the M62, south on the M1. Old Maggie was right. She nearly always was. It was a case with odd aspects and Roper's should have come ahead of it. Roper's paid over the odds for a good fast job. It was a stock fraud, costly computer gear, and the stock fraud hadn't been dreamt up Crane couldn't figure out. But stock frauds were boring. And Jane Kennedy had got instincts going in him that had lately been on hold. Being him, he knew he now had to know more.

From the M1 he arced off on to the Orbital and at junction eleven on to the A320. It was a winding road that led through tunnels of lush woodland. Hadn't he read somewhere about Surrey and its leafy lanes? He was used to open moorland, not a tree in sight. He came to a big roundabout which put him on a road leading to the centre of Woking. He located the canal and the car-park next to it off Brewery Road. He paid and displayed for three hours.

It had been a day of ragged cloud on the way down, with showers, but the weather was more settled now and he crossed the road in clear light. He walked quickly through a modern complex of walkways and malls, built round the pedestrian zone of an open square. It was busy by now: shoppers, people handing out flyers, men who shouted the prices of fruit and vegetables piled on stalls. He came out at the top of a narrow alleyway opposite the railway station. He went through the underpass and Eastern Lane was just beyond the station forecourt. Jane Kennedy had been right, parking everywhere was near impossible, with yellow lines on parts of Eastern Lane itself.

He'd dressed himself carefully in a dark-blue lightweight suit, white shirt and striped tie, and carried a document case. The house in question was a substantial semi in good condition, with a well-tended front garden. He rang the door-bell, ready with carefully-honed spiel if anyone actually opened the door. But no one did and he tried the adjoining semi. After a lengthy pause, the door was opened by a tired-looking woman with lank fair hair, dressed in jeans and a long sweater. A little girl stood at her side, who watched Crane with unblinking curiosity. A baby yelled in the background.

Crane dug out his most disarming smile. 'Oh dear, you seem to have your hands full.'

She eyed him guardedly. 'I'm not buying anything,' she said. 'We might be able to afford double-glazing in 2010 but don't get your hopes up.'

Crane acted a chuckle. 'Let me put your mind at rest. I was trying to contact Mrs Powell, but she looks to be out. I'm from the council. There was a query about her Council Tax — '

'About the banding?' the woman cut him off. 'It's not just Mrs Powell, we're all convinced these houses are in the wrong one.'

That was handy. 'I'd better not go into it until I've spoken to Mrs Powell. Would you know if she'll be long? Perhaps I could call back after lunch.'

The little girl said, 'I'm having a party for my birthday with a bouncy castle *and* a slide. But I'm not inviting Kirstie Stott.'

'Don't you, dear.' Crane clipped back on his crinkly smile. 'I've heard she spoils things.'

'Daddy gets so cross. She touches all the sandwiches . . . '

The young woman raised her eyebrows, smiled. She seemed to be taking in Crane's decent clothes and deceptively open looks. 'Mrs Powell . . . she's not been well. Nervous trouble. She's been stressed out for months. She's in Brookfield, but please don't bother

her there. She should be back in a couple of weeks, I believe.'

'Oh, I'm so sorry. It's really nothing that won't wait. I do hope she makes a full recovery.'

The woman watched him in another brief silence. 'Well, I'm sure you know what put her in there. I doubt she'll ever be over it. I know I shouldn't.'

He nodded slowly. If he was pretending to be a local man he had to pretend he knew what had given Dora Powell nervous trouble. He didn't want to say anything for the woman to remember him by. He'd be able to get it together later.

'Well, look, if Mrs Powell has been so ill I'd not mention I called, it might add to her anxiety. I'll get back to her in a month or so.'

She nodded absently. The baby in the background was screaming now with a noise like a steam whistle. Crane, not knowing much about babies, wondered how its head didn't explode.

'I'm having a cake with six candles on.' The little girl's voice followed him gravely along the drive. 'And a little balleriny . . .'

★ ★ ★

30

Gordy's hand shook a little. He never liked speaking to Lenny, not even over the phone. He was beginning to wish to Christ he was out of it all. Lenny said, 'Yes,' softly.

'There's a geezer been there now, Lenny, then he went next door and he's rabbiting on to the woman with the kids.'

'What does he look like?'

'Tall, over six, fair hair, blue suit. Tatchy-case. Looks kind of official.'

'Has he been to any other houses?'

'Just the two.'

'Tell Wayne to get moving. And tell Wayne if he loses him he'd better lose himself.'

'Right you are, Lenny.'

'Leg it, Wayne,' he said, clearing the phone. 'He's just leaving the bird with the kids. Keep Lenny up to speed every foot of the way this time, cause he'll be in his car now and waiting. And make sure you get his fucking *number*, cause Lenny says if you was to lose him you'll be back south of the river. For good.'

'Fuck it,' Wayne muttered. 'It won't be *nothing*. He'll be selling kitchens. I tell you, Gordy, I'd have Donny back tomorrow even if he did go off his loaf a bit now and then.'

Gordy sighed. Wouldn't they all?

★ ★ ★

31

Back in the centre, Crane asked his way to the Post Office, looked at a classified. There was no hospital listed under Brookfield; he tried nursing homes: there was a Brookfield Clinic. It discreetly advised that sympathetic help and treatment could be given in cases of depression and stress, alcoholism and eating disorders. Out-patient care, day care and residential care. He rang. 'I'd like to visit a Mrs Dora Powell,' he said. 'Do you have set visiting times?'

'Who's speaking, please?'

'Just a family friend.'

'Could I call you back, sir, when I've made sure Mrs Powell is well enough to receive a visitor? I'm sorry, but the nature of our care facilities, we have to ask for your co-operation. I'm sure you understand.'

In other words they didn't want some arsehole of a reporter sneaking his way in and finding out which model or pop-star was having the latest detox.

'I quite understand,' he said. 'Look, I've got an urgent call coming through on my mobile. If I could contact you again shortly with all my details . . . '

He pocketed the phone with a wry smile. It had been a piece of piss, and the case was now closed. He crossed the main city road, but before claiming his car he went along the canal bank a short way. He sat on a bench to eat a sandwich he'd bought and to drink coffee from a lidded plastic cup. This was a good area, especially in sunlight. The path was dappled in tree cover and the houses across the canal had gardens that extended to the water's edge. Some of them had boats moored at little jetties. He could see the big beasts, when they got back from the city, having drinks in tall glasses on shady patios.

There'd be a library somewhere or a newspaper office, where he could have studied back numbers. If people generally knew what had caused Dora Powell so much grief it had to have been reported to the local press. But he'd have to set aside a couple of hours and he wanted to be back on the road now before the traffic build-up of the late afternoon.

Serious car accident? Horrific break-in? An attempted rape? Those were the stress-makers you read about. And maybe Jane was involved and maybe not. But it was Jane he couldn't get off his mind and not what had put Dora in Brookfield. Woking looked to be a clean, attractive town to live and work in and her lover lived here, so why had she left it to go 250 miles up the road to an industrial relic of a textile city? Then chosen to live on an estate even Bradford people barely knew existed?

And he'd never bought it that she was so snowed under with work that she couldn't spare a day to find out what he'd found out, and just as easily. Crane tossed his empty cup and sandwich wrapper in a waste-bin and made for Brewery Road. He shrugged. There'd be some banal explanation to it all, there always was. He had a feeling that in this case the truth might keep its tantalizing glow from being uncovered.

Crane had cleared the M25 and was twenty minutes along the M1 when he sensed he was being tailed. Watching his back was an ingrained reflex that went back to a time when he'd had to watch it very carefully. The dark-blue Vauxhall was always somewhere behind him. Never directly behind, but always around, two or three cars back. He'd shadowed many cars in the past and knew the dodges.

'Can't be,' he muttered, shaking his head. Why should anyone be tailing *him*? How could they even know who he was or what he was doing? He'd not been doing much anyway. Finding out why a woman wasn't at home. It made no sense. Sooner or later the Vauxhall would pull off the motorway, or speed up and pass him and that would be that.

But it didn't. Crane tried a couple of

moves. He pulled in to the near-side lane and dropped his speed. The Vauxhall gradually fell back till it was almost out of sight. Then Crane hit the throttle, driving as fast as he dared for the next five miles. By then he looked to have lost the other car completely. But when he cut back to his normal speed the Vauxhall distantly appeared in his rear-view mirror. Which meant he'd copied Crane's manoeuvre exactly. Assuming it was a he. It would be.

He drove on steadily past the patchwork of farmland fields on the edges of towns and villages. Names dropped off signboards: Hemel Hempstead, Harpenden, Luton, Newport Pagnell, the motorway filling or calming as major routes merged from the west. The blue car was always there, in the thick of it all.

He had to have been followed from Woking. Why? And *how*? He'd been on foot most of the time, looking like some suit from an office. He scoured his trained memory. He'd eaten his sandwich on the canal bank and there'd been a few strollers, mainly old folk and one or two couples hand in hand. A young bloke on the canal bridge, mobile to his ear, in his own world. No one who'd stood out. And he'd not clocked the Vauxhall on the road from Woking to the Orbital. But the cars behind had been strung out in line as it wasn't the sort of twisty road to risk overtaking on.

At least he had the Vauxhall's number. It had been just close enough at one point for him to catch it. He'd talk Benson into running it through the NC for him and find out who it was registered to. He could then think what he'd do about it. He decided on one final test to make absolutely certain the bloke really was on his tail. He drew abreast of a string of petrol tankers, trundling almost nose to tail like elephants at a steady sixty. Just before he'd begun to pass them he'd clocked a sign that indicated a service area at the next turn-off. He put his foot down, reached the head of the convoy, and just had the leeway to dart across the leader's bows and on to the slip-road. He drove as rapidly as possible through the busy car-park and beyond the complex that housed the shops and diners, in the direction of the exit route. The track widened here to include a petrol station and an area for truck parking, and there was enough space to pull in without blocking other vehicles. He got out then and looked carefully through fold-up binoculars across the coloured tops of the rows of cars, glinting in sunlight, to the distant narrow entrance allotted to saloons. To see, inside a minute, the blue Vauxhall nose its way cautiously from it.

Crane got back in his car and drove off to rejoin the motorway. By the time the Vauxhall had checked out all those parked vehicles he'd be too far along the M1 to be caught up. The bloke wouldn't even know he was still on it. But he'd have caught on by then that Crane definitely knew he'd been shadowed.

And what could he do about it then? Zilch. But Crane wasn't happy.

3

Crane was back in Bradford to catch Benson at the Toll Gate. He was smoking heavily as usual.

'Do me a favour?' he asked reluctantly.

'Another number through the ringer? I'm not keen, Frank.'

'Oh, come on, Ted, for Christ's sake. Who's to know? And you know I can find it anyway, if I lay the notes out.'

The other sighed. 'What's the story?'

'I wish I knew. This Jane Kennedy you put me on to. Missing pal in Woking. Well, I was down there today and sorted it. Only now some arsehole in a blue Vauxhall tried to trail me north.'

'Why would he do that?'

'I don't know that either.'

Benson watched him through the smoke. 'If it starts to look dodgy you'd better let us know.'

'If it does I will,' Crane said shortly.

'The bloke must have *your* number. You had thought of that? And maybe *he* knows someone who can access the NC.'

'I got lucky. I used the Woking trip to get

38

my own car serviced. They lent me a spare at the dealers, one of those old Renault Nineteens they don't do now.'

'So if he *could* place the number it would only take him to the Renault place?'

Crane nodded. 'It keeps me anonymous. Even so, I'll be wanting answers from Miss Kennedy.'

'He followed you from Woking? Maybe it's some nutter of a boyfriend trying to track her down.'

'You could be right. Except that all the signs seem to point to any love interest that's going on is between Jane and the Woking woman, name of Dora Powell.'

'What a waste of good totty.'

'Christ knows how the bloke picked me up.'

'Maybe he was watching Dora's house.'

'Makes no sense. How could he watch it twenty-four seven? You'll run that number for me?' He handed Benson one of his cards with the number written on.

'I suppose so.'

'I'll be seeing you.'

Crane finished his drink and left. He didn't like asking Benson for anything these days. But Benson owed him, owed him on a grand scale. And when people owed you a debt they were never going to be able to repay it led to a tense relationship. And it killed gratitude overnight.

★ ★ ★

He stood again at the door of the small detached. Two little girls played in a distant garden, an elderly man clipped a hedge. The only signs of life on a sunny evening. He waited, knowing she'd be looking through the viewing glass. He turned to give her the full mug-shot, heard the bolts and deadlocks sliding back.

'Hello again, Frank.' She gave him the usual lost smile, led him into the same room as before. The view through the patio door had been blurred by rain and low cloud the first time he'd called, he now saw it clearly. The garden backed on to woodland and beyond it rising green-belt terrain. It added to the cut-off feeling you got when you drove on to Blackbird Common.

'There's *some* bad news,' he told her, 'but it's mainly good.'

She became still, her eyes widening. She'd not wanted to know any of it over the phone, had asked him to come to the house, almost brusquely. He sensed she'd guessed he'd not be using a landline. If so, did that mean she was guarding her privacy to the point of paranoia?

'Your friend's had some nervous trouble. She's being looked after in a place called the Brookfield Clinic. According to her neighbour she'll be there maybe another week or so.'

'You didn't give the neighbour any idea — '

'I'm an experienced PI, for Christ's sake.'

She started, as if he'd slapped her. He shouldn't have been so curt. Even so, the kid was too touchy to say she worked in a commercial office.

'I'm sorry, I didn't mean . . . You're the expert, of course.' Her eyes left his. 'So *that's* it, a breakdown. Poor darling. Things have been so difficult for her. Not just our bust-up. I do wish there was something I could do.'

He gave her a leaf from his notebook. 'The name, the number. They screen callers very carefully.'

Her eyes met his again. 'I'll give my name; see if she'll speak to me.' There was a sudden catch in her husky voice. 'Poor darling Dora.'

'The neighbour strongly hinted at some past crisis,' Crane said evenly.

The old wariness fell into place. 'She's had a bad couple of years. And with Harry leaving her . . . they'd been together an awful long time.'

'The neighbour also gave the impression

41

Dora had had the sort of trouble that gets into the press.'

Two spots of colour burned in her pale cheeks. Crane had seen them once before, the first time he was here. 'Oh dear,' she said, in a voice that was slow, uneasy and meant she was searching for the right words. 'I wonder what it could have been. She never mentioned anything. Perhaps she didn't want to worry me. The neighbour, she didn't give any indication . . . ?'

She was now watching Crane very closely. 'None.'

Her shoulders sagged slightly. It had to be an easing of tension. They sat in the same armchairs as before, though the gas-fire was unlit and the room looked slightly more attractive in bands of evening sunlight, though not much. 'Thank you, Frank,' she said then, 'for such a fast, efficient job. I'll ring the Brookfield this evening.'

He could tell by her tone and manner she felt the case had been brought to its logical end.

'There's more,' he said flatly. 'Someone tried to follow my car from Woking. Don't worry, I lost him.'

That lit the blue touchpaper. Her mouth fell open. He could see the whites round the irises of eyes wide with shock. She couldn't get a word out for several long seconds and when she did her voice was a near-croak. 'You were followed? *Followed*. How could you have been? How could you *possibly* have been?'

'I was hoping you might be able to tell me.'

She stared at him again in another stunned silence. 'How should *I* know?' she suddenly cried. 'How could I *possibly* know?'

'Because you know a whole lot more about all this than you're letting on.'

She shook her head, repeatedly. 'I don't know what you mean. I told you everything you needed to know.'

'That's the trouble: seems all I needed to know was half a story.'

'But . . . but . . . anything else is my private business. I simply wanted to know where Dora *was*.' She spoke now in a low distracted voice and it was clear to Crane she was struggling to get her mind round what he'd sprung on her.

'I can see that. But when people begin shadowing my car it becomes my business too. It was a blue Vauxhall. You've no idea who might have been in it?'

'None at all.' She shook her head again violently. 'Absolutely none at all.'

'Why did you really leave Woking, Jane?'

There was a sudden haunted shadow in her

amber eyes. 'I told you. A job I wanted — '

'You leave your best friend, bust-up or no bust-up, to come all this way north. They must have FAs in wealthy attractive towns like Woking and Guildford who could have given you what you're getting here.'

'I've explained all that — '

'And why do you shut yourself up in a place like Blackbird Common?'

'It's all I could get at the *time*! Don't you think I'd like a decent flat near the city?'

Crane had read a lot of faces. He wondered which emotion came out front in the confusion showing in hers: fear, guilt, anger.

'You do know what happened to Dora, don't you, that brought on the nervous breakdown. What was your involvement?'

'But I *don't* know. I left Surrey ages ago — '

'Because of Harry walking out on Dora? Why was that? Was Harry losing it because of what was going on between you and her? Did that lead to some kind of violence?'

'I don't know what you mean. Please leave it, Frank, just leave it.'

'You were lovers, weren't you, you and Dora? None of my business, I couldn't care less. But could that have been Harry on my tail?'

'Stop!' she cried. She closed her eyes as

though she had a splitting headache. 'You sound like the fucking *police*!'

'I once was the police,' he said harshly. He wished he'd not said it the second the words were out.

He'd handed her another shock. Not as bad as the shock over the blue Vauxhall, but it was there, behind the mute, veiled look she gave him. It was unlikely he'd ever have got much from her before. It was certain now.

After another of those long silences he was growing used to she finally broke it. 'I need a drink,' she said, in a low voice. 'You?'

He nodded reluctantly. 'A small one. Gin and tonic, if you have it.'

She went off. He'd been working instinctively to old rhythms, hadn't wanted her to have time to think. He had to remind himself he'd not been police for a long time and was now a PI. And PIs had to respect client confidentiality. They had to do what they were told by whoever paid the ferryman. He had no problem with that normally, but this hadn't been a normal job.

He glanced around the room. How could she live in a place like this? It reminded him of his granny's. A suite in two-tone green moquette, a faded, patterned carpet, chocolate-box pictures set too high, a small teak dining-table against the back wall that had four unmatching straight-back chairs. Did *anyone* ever come to dinner? He had to go easy on the kid. He knew he was beginning to feel sorry for her, but the way he was coming across he doubted she ever would.

She came back with the drinks. They both looked to be the same. She wore more casual clothes than the other night: a sleeveless fitted shirt in grey silk and dark-silver trousers slightly flared. She'd drawn her thick wavy hair back into a pony-tail. This time Crane could see no trace of her true colouring beneath the chestnut tint. He guessed she'd spotted those tell-tale blonde roots herself and done some touching up. So she'd not stand out in a crowd?

'Thanks.' He picked up his glass from a battered tin tray that had a picture of Paddington Bear on it.

'Frank . . . '

'I know, I was well out of line. Blame it on my once being a copper.'

She gave him a small wan smile. 'You came over so cold, so professional.'

There was a note in her voice that could have been longing. She sounded like a woman who wanted something from him that couldn't be bought with a cheque.

'Look, Jane, I didn't mean to go on at you.

Your life's your own. But you are my client and while you are I have a duty to you to make sure you're not in any danger. Now this man in the Vauxhall, he can have no interest in me personally. He can only be following me to find some way of contacting *you*. And I can't let that happen.'

She began to swallow and her eyes were moist. She got up and crossed to the window, where her ripening body was almost a silhouette against the declining light. She stood motionless in another stretching silence. Crane got up himself and moved towards her. Tears ran steadily down her pale cheeks. He took out a handkerchief, passed it to her.

He said, 'Who are you running from? I'll try to help. If I can't handle it I'll take it to Benson, the DS who gave you my name.'

She mopped her eyes with the handkerchief, rubbed her wet cheek with the back of a hand, took a deep breath. 'You're right, Frank,' she said at last in a shaky voice, 'I've got problems. I'd give anything to tell you the truth, but it's just not possible. It really isn't, believe me. You couldn't begin to guess at my trouble. And I'm really in no danger, not even if you *were* followed. It must seem difficult to believe when I seemed so upset, but it's true.' She swallowed again. 'But thank you so much for caring.'

She put out a hand towards him. It was an involuntary gesture and she abruptly drew it back. But Crane put his own hand over it anyway, and pressed it.

'All right,' he said, 'it's your life and you know best. But, well, don't hesitate to contact me if you ever think you might need help. I'm only a phone call away and I'm nearly always around. If you can't get me on the mobile ring the office. There's an old girl called Maggie who does a couple of hours a day for me, setting up the diary and doing the invoices. When she's not there the calls are rerouted to her own phone. She's discreet and reliable.'

She nodded, drawing her hand slowly from his. 'I can't tell you how glad I am about Dora, the way you sorted it. I'll ring her this evening.' She broke off, then said hesitantly, 'Please don't take this the wrong way, I know you're a pro, but . . . you don't think whoever was in the Vauxhall made a note of your car's number?'

'It wouldn't do him any good,' he told her, then explained about having driven to Woking in a courtesy car.

'I'm so glad,' she said, her shoulders sinking in relief as before. 'That was lucky.'

'PIs sometimes need luck,' he said. But she was a sharp one. She seemed to know that

48

there were people apart from the police who had ways of accessing the National Computer.

'I hope I'll not have to turn to you again, but . . . if you'd like to come by for a drink some time — ' She broke off, suddenly confused. 'Oh, what am I *saying*. You've got your own life, of course you have. I really didn't mean . . . I just meant — '

He smiled. 'That you're a stranger in a strange city and Blackbird Common's not the friendliest of places. I'd like to. I'll give you a call one evening. It'll be lateish. I work long days.'

'Any time,' she said, in a small, strained voice. 'I'm always at home.'

He knew.

She saw him to the door, watched him go to his car as before. It was almost a yearning to be able to tell him the real truth. She was positive she could trust him, even if he had once been police, with contacts still in the force. She turned away sadly. But she knew it wasn't fair to involve him; it could lead to problems, and she'd already got more than she could handle. She'd already taken too much of a chance, and now look what had happened. Not that she could see *how* it had happened, that at least was the truth. Someone must have been watching Dora's. But that made no sense either. She hoped

Frank *would* come for a drink. She smiled faintly. He'd have a partner, maybe even a wife; everyone had of his age, what would it be, mid-thirties? But he'd not see her as any kind of a threat, because he thought she and Dora had been lovers. She hoped he'd come. Just to have his strong, reassuring presence, to feel that smile he was so stingy with giving her such a lift. He was a tough bastard. But then, she'd always had a soft spot for tough bastards.

She drifted back to the dining-room. She'd make herself a meal and have a glass or two of wine. She'd try hard again to look forward, to move on. That's what they'd said she had to make herself try to do. She didn't want another of those frightening black-outs which only seemed to come when she began to think of the old times.

★   ★   ★

The phone rang early in his office.

'Crane.'

'It's Ted. The Vauxhall. It's registered to a company not an individual. D.C. Properties Ltd, Woking address. Seems koscher.'

'Means nothing to me, but thanks.'

'You saw the woman last evening? What did *she* make of it?'

50

'Nothing worth shit, but she knows more than she gives out.' He gave Benson a brief rundown of the situation between Jane, Dora and Harry. 'I have an idea this Harry character might be at the bottom of it.'

'Could be there's a restraining order on him,' Benson said. 'He could have caused so much aggro in the past she decided to get as far away from Woking as she could.'

'And maybe he's been trying to pin her down ever since.'

'This lesbian carry-on, could be she's a fiver each way. Maybe the Dora woman to start with and then getting hooked on Harry.'

'The thought had crossed my own mind. It could explain the bust-up with Dora and Harry trying to track her down.'

'Sounds a funny old fuck-up,' Benson said. 'But in our line of work you get funny old fuck-ups once a week.'

Crane put down the phone. It would explain why she was frightened, but not exactly terrified. Maybe this Harry could cause a lot of trouble but wasn't dangerous, just a pest. And maybe she could alert the Woking Bill if she felt he really was trying to harass her again, and they'd send someone round to his place to tell him to cool it. It might explain why she'd buried herself up here.

He wondered if he would call and see her again. Perhaps best to let things lie. She was certainly fanciable even if she was maybe a fiver each way. He felt genuinely sorry for her though he knew what a dodgy emotion it was to have around a client. She looked as if she'd had a really bad time, the sort of time that comes close to breaking your spirit. But there was some kind of fight still there, he'd seen a flash of it when they'd been going head to head. Well, there'd been no one in his life since Vicky, and Vicky being Vicky there was no one who was ever going to take her place. But just now and then he liked being with an attractive woman.

★ ★ ★

Mike Beesley's phone rang. 'It's the police again, Mike, someone called Chapman.'

'Put him on, Dee Dee.'

'Mr Beesley? I'm detective sergeant Michael Chapman. I'm with the Guildford police, sir.'

'Guildford? Is that where it's turned up?'

'I'm sorry?'

'We are talking a stolen Laguna?'

'No, sir, this is another matter and much more serious. I'm involved in a highly confidential investigation and it's very important I know who was driving a Renault Nineteen, shown as belonging to yourselves, Jarvis Motors, yesterday afternoon between Woking and Bradford.'

Beesley thought for a few seconds. They had only one Nineteen left now among the spares. He was pretty sure it had been loaned out to Frank Crane. Crane had been in with his own Renault for servicing yesterday, Beesley knew, as he'd seen him at Service Reception and gone out to have a word with him.

'I'm sorry,' he said, 'but that's confidential information.'

'Mr Beesley,' the other said evenly, 'I'm a police detective.'

'I'm sorry,' Beesley said again, 'but I don't know you from Joe Bloggs.'

'You don't need to,' the other said, in a curter tone, 'you just take my word. I've had people on this case for weeks and I need the information urgently. So you either help me or I'm going to have to think about charging you with obstructing a police enquiry.'

'Charge away,' Beesley said, in a similarly curt tone, 'but you only get the info if I get the ID. You've got two choices: either fax me on an official letterhead, or you get someone in the Bradford police to OK it. I can give you a contact.'

'There's no time, Mr Beesley, I've got

people standing by now waiting for this information and all it needs is a name — '

'The answer's still no. It's confidential customer information and I don't release it without ID.'

'Look, Beesley — '

'Don't Beesley me, mate. You don't get it without backing and that's that. You could be the bloke cleaning the lavs for all I know.'

'All right, you arsehole, but believe me you're putting yourself in deep serious shit.'

'Tell me about it. You're in deep serious shit every other fucking day in the motor trade.'

A distant phone was abruptly cut off.

★ ★ ★

A hands-free phone sounded in Crane's car. 'Crane.'

'Mike Beesley, Frank. That old Nineteen we lent you yesterday. Some bloke making out he was the Guildford Bill rang wanting to know who was driving it between Woking and here yesterday afternoon.'

'Did you tell him?'

'No chance. I only let that kind of info out to bobbies I know and trust. But in any case this bloke seemed kind of iffy. He was not happy. You got trouble?'

'No. I was followed for part of the way from Woking, but I lost whoever it was on the Ml. I'm certain it's something to do with a case I'm working on.'

'There's been no follow-up. I tried 1471. Nothing. Do you think it *could* have been the police? He obviously had access to the number cruncher.'

'I don't know, Mike. It sounds iffy, as you say.'

'We have it on tape if you want to listen. We tape the lot these days. Cuts out the aggro. If we have to replace a cambelt we need proof the punter was warned the size hole it was going to burn in his pocket.'

'I'd like to listen. I can't say too much, but it's a funny case I'm working on.'

'No prob. Maybe you'd like to look at the latest Megane while you're here . . . off the transporter this very morning.'

Crane smiled wryly, drove on. Like all dedicated car and insurance salesmen, Beesley could never be accused of missing a trick. He drove to the Renault showroom as soon as he could find a window in his tight schedule. Beesley took him in his office. He was tall, well knit and had a head of dark, luxuriant hair. Behind the ever-friendly smile he was as tough as you had to be in the car business, but the deals if hard were always fair. Crane was glad Beesley had handled the call from the so-called DS Chapman. Someone less street-wise might have let the information go. The tape had been removed from the phone system, and Beesley slotted it into a monitor.

'Look, Mike, I don't want to give you any trouble. Take my word, neither me or your motor are out of line with the police. And I'm as much in the dark as you are.'

'Not to fret, old son. Christ, they don't come much straighter than you. Anyway, get your Britneys going on this . . .'

'Mind if I record your recording?'

'Be my guest.'

Crane set his micro-cassette going at the side of the monitor, listened carefully. He had to hand it to the man, if he was an impostor he had the flat tone and used the sort of formal language police did use with this kind of request, at least initially. The voice was firm and classless, but he spoke with the long A of the south-east.

'Definitely an impostor,' he said, when the tape had spooled to its end. 'A trained policeman wouldn't have lost his cool, not if co-operation was so vital. Police will always *try* to get info over the phone, but they have to provide authorization if you request it.'

'And there's been none forthcoming.'

Crane got up. 'Well, thanks, Mike, thanks a lot. I don't know what's going on, but don't worry, I'll sort it. The last thing I want is to give you any trouble with my affairs.'

'Forget it. The sort of game you're in you're bound to come across some dodgy characters now and then.' He grinned. 'Just like the car trade. I'll see you out.'

But that was so he could walk Crane past a gleaming maroon Megane. 'This car has your name on it, Frank. Metallic paint, ABS, airbags, air con, power steering, electric sun-roof, immobilizer. And your *sound* system . . . '

'I'll think about it.'

'Don't think too long, old son. If I was to offer the deal I can offer you, as an old friend, to anyone else, this car would be gone in an hour.'

Crane grinned. In his dreams. Preoccupied, he got back in his own car, waved to Beesley, edged out on to the city road. How had the pretend-policeman got into the NC without inside help? He'd have to have a contact. Like Crane himself. Could that make him a PI too?

4

'Nick? Frank Crane.'

'Frank, hi there! How's Bradford? Dark and satanic as ever?'

'I keep telling you, it's a different place now. They've sandblasted all the mills and turned them into B & Qs.'

'I'd love to come up there sometime, but they say you need a working knowledge of Urdu to get around.'

Crane rolled his eyes in resignation. 'Look, Nick, do you know of any decent agents in the Woking area?'

'No. I'm not saying there aren't any good ones, just that I've never needed to find out. Surrey's close enough for me not to lay anything off. Can *I* help?'

Crane hesitated. Gardner was good but he was expensive, London-based expensive. Gardner said, 'You'd have a problem passing on the costs?'

'I'd not be able to pass them on at all. I've got a funny case.'

'What do you need?'

Crane gave him a brief version of the story of Jane and Dora. 'Something happened to

Dora that may have involved Jane, something big enough to get it into the local press. I'm worried about any possible blowbacks; it's as much about my reputation as the client's. I'm certain I could have found out if I'd gone through back numbers. I wish I'd done that now.'

Gardner was silent for a few seconds. 'Well, look,' he said, 'I'll do you a budget-price job if it's just a question of checking out newspapers. Woking's only half an hour from London on a fast train. I could clear it up in three hours tops, I should think.'

'I'd appreciate it, Nick. When do you think?'

'That's the not so good news. I'm looking at my diary as we speak . . . four days soonest.'

It was disappointing, but if PIs weren't working their bollocks off they were no bloody good. 'That'll do me. And thanks, Nick. I owe you one.'

He put down the phone. The expense didn't hurt him too badly. He made a good living. Didn't do holidays, didn't have a family to support, had no expensive hobbies. He knew Jane wasn't going to tell him what had happened to Dora, or maybe to Dora and her, but it was now becoming a piece of the jigsaw he felt he had to have. It might give him some definite info about the situation she was in. He was still very uneasy about being followed on the motorway, and this call Beesley had received didn't help. If this Harry type *was* involved, he might be turning into a bit more than just a bloody pest. He could have brooded himself into a state of being dangerous. It happened. Crane had decided he couldn't take the risk. Not now he'd got to know her, seen the state she was in. And he really did have to think about his agency. Couldn't do with anything getting in the papers, the very worst kind of publicity for a man who lived by his anonymity.

★ ★ ★

'Hello,' she said, in that cool, wary tone he was getting to know so well.

'It's me, Jane, Frank.'

'Oh . . . hello, Frank.'

'I'm through for the day. I thought maybe I could take you up on that offer of a drink.'

'I'd like that.' There was a pause. 'Have you eaten? I could give you a meal, if you like.'

'Don't go to any trouble.'

'It'll only be M & S take-away.'

'How did you know they're what I live on?'

That was handy. If she had a drink or two, maybe some wine, she might feel she could unbend a little and trust him. That aside, it would be good to spend a little quality time with an attractive woman who had a slight cast in her amber eyes that made her even more of a turn-on. He'd long accepted he was sod-all to look at, but he had the feeling she'd quite taken to him, even though he'd not given her an easy ride. He'd decided he had to help her sort things out, even though she insisted she was in no real danger. He wondered what that meant exactly. He drove on to Blackbird Common, along the lengthy road that ended in that oblong cul-de-sac. A handful of cars stood in drives or on the roadside, but he could see no life at all this evening, Christ, it was like that ancient pop song he'd heard on the car radio earlier in the day, 'Everyone's Gone to the Moon'.

The bolts and deadlocks were sliding back as he got to the door. She'd been waiting for him. She was carefully made up and her chestnut-tinted hair shone with brushing. She wore a dark-green shift dress of some material with a slight sheen.

'Hello, Frank.' Her smile was warmer now but still didn't get through to her sad eyes. She took him through to the usual room. It seemed almost festive this evening. She'd spread a clean white cloth on the dining-table and laid it with cutlery and wine glasses. A bottle of white wine stood chilling in a gel-filled jacket. An occasional table stood on the old hearth-rug with drinks glasses, gin, tonics and ice in a vacuum container.

'I did say not to go to any trouble.'

'It's as simple to cook for two as for one. Is Chinese all right?'

'Chinese sounds great. Mind if I take my jacket off?'

'You do have the look of a man who's happier in shirt sleeves.'

She made up the gins and tonic and they sat on the same armchairs as before. 'Thanks for coming,' she said simply, as she handed him his glass. 'I haven't really managed to make too many friends since I got here.'

'It takes time,' he said. 'Have you been able to speak to your Woking friend, at least?'

'Oh, yes. She's a lot better. She was glad to talk. I'm so pleased.'

She sounded it too.

'Good. Will she be able to go home soon?'

'She's been told she can think of going as soon as she feels able to come to terms — ' She broke off. 'Come to terms with life in the outside world again. That . . . that was how they put it.'

Crane didn't think it was. He was guessing they'd told Dora she could go when she'd come to terms with what had put her there in the first place.

'I suppose you must have lived in Woking for some time yourself,' he said casually. He knew it had to be casual if he was going to get anything at all out of her about that big blank space she'd made of her near-past.

'The best part of a year.' She glanced down into her glass. It was quiet enough to hear the ice snapping. Maybe it was to remind herself not to let the Gordon's loosen her tongue. 'I worked in Kent till I was twenty. I was born there. Ashford.'

'What made you leave?'

She glanced through the window at the darkening back garden. 'I sometimes wish I hadn't.' Crane heard a brooding note in her husky voice.

'Because of Dora? The bust-up?'

Her eyes had an unfocused, preoccupied look then. 'That . . . that was part of it,' she finally admitted. 'But so much changed. I had all my friends in Ashford, people I'd known since schooldays.' She suddenly gave him an almost open smile. 'We ran a bit wild, I suppose. Pubs, clubs, Karaoke. Summer weekends when we'd go to the coast and get rat-arsed on the beach. Christmases when we'd do the booze-run to France. We were all as daft as a brush, that's what you say in the north, isn't it, always shrieking with laughter, but it was such a lot of *fun*.'

For a short time she was living the old days as she talked. It was like seeing a different Jane. But it was a Jane he'd always sensed was there, hidden inside the one who dyed her blonde hair brown and wore quiet clothes and locked herself carefully away in a dismal house on a dismal estate.

'But why *did* you leave?' he asked again. 'If you were enjoying life so much.'

She came reluctantly out of a past that seemed to have been shot in colour to a present that was now in grainy black and white. She looked at him as if she'd almost forgotten he was there. 'Oh.' She shrugged. 'Job prospects. The money was good. I thought it was time I began looking after myself, branching out. It was too easy at home, and I was getting too used to it.'

But she'd used a well-paid job as the reason for moving to Bradford too, and it didn't ring true this time either.

'And Dora took you under her wing . . . '

She raised her eyebrows slightly, smiled, nodded. 'I'd better have a look at the food. It should be about ready.'

He got up when she'd gone, glass in hand, and crossed to the window. The setting sun was cutting deep shadows into the uneven rising land beyond the back garden and the woodland. He reckoned he could stop digging around, booze or no booze. It was second nature to her now, keeping the cards very close.

He would have to tell her about Mike Beesley's call from the pretend-policeman. That was the main reason he'd wanted to come here tonight. She had to be warned that whoever it was he wasn't giving up so easily. But not yet. Let her eat her dinner in peace. His company couldn't be much but she seemed to be enjoying it, at least enjoying it as much as a woman could who was weighed down with such a heavy load of emotional baggage.

She ate a lot. Not greedily, but steadily. It was the sort of meal where a number of small dishes were laid out, of saffron rice and noodles and bamboo shoots, together with the prawns and the slivers of duckling, pork and lamb. Crane always ate sparingly, to keep himself in trim for the long days, but with Chinese food it wasn't difficult to give an impression he was eating his share. It was as he'd guessed, food was a comfort for her in her unhappiness, the food and the Entre-deux-Mers. Before long her attractive curves were going to balloon if she couldn't find an answer to what had stopped life being the bunch of fun it had been in Ashford.

They talked generally, as the main course gave way to cherry tart with cream and then cheese. She told him a little about the financial services work she did, which all seemed authentic, and he told her about the sort of work PIs did: the life-style checks, the bad debt recovery, the money wealthy types being sued for divorce buried in off-shore accounts.

Crane had taken only one glass of wine because of the driving. She had had maybe three but they'd done nothing to loosen her tongue. She said no more about her past, and gave an impression she wished she'd said nothing at all. She began to clear the table.

'Need any help with the washing up?'

'No, thanks all the same. There's a dish-washer. Bog-standard but it does the job.'

She came back with cups and a jug of coffee on a tray.

'I enjoyed the meal. Thanks a lot.'

'I enjoyed the company, Frank.'

He drank some coffee. She finished her last glass of wine. He wished now he'd turned down the offer of a meal. It didn't go with the new piece of bad news he had to hand her. But he'd been tempted. He'd not been near an attractive woman in months. Maybe she'd been tempted in the same way, just to have a bloke around the place for a couple of hours, even him. And maybe in both cases it hadn't been a good idea.

'Look,' he said, 'the last thing I want is to cast a damper on the evening, but I have to tell you this. Someone *did* take the number of the Renault Nineteen I went to Woking in and they managed to run it through the National Computer. This man then pretended to be a police detective, rang the Renault place and tried to find out who was driving it.'

The hand holding the wine-glass began to quiver. Her sudden pallor showed through the blusher. He'd handed her another jolt and she was frightened. But it wasn't the wide-eyed shock of last time. She seemed to watch him in the table-lamp's glow with a kind of resignation, even a sort of fatalism. It puzzled him. Like everything else about her.

'So . . . he's got your name,' she said, in a near-whisper.

'No. Beesley refused to give it to him without proper authorization. There wasn't any.'

★　★　★

Its real name was The Tavern, but it had come to be known as The Glass-house. There was glass everywhere. The chandeliers dripped glittering shards of it, the tables were made of it, there were frosted-glass panels in the cubicle dividers, and the bar itself was backed by a single great mirror. Adam stood near the wall, away from the bar, alone. He could have had plenty of company. The Glass-house had always attracted a fair number of gays, who appreciated the kitschy atmosphere and the Abba songs and the Judy Garland ballads. But ever since the stranger had walked in he'd sensed he was being looked at. He was used to it. He only had to glance in one of the many mirrors to see he was looking his best: slender, corn-coloured hair, blue eyes, well-shaped features. Nicely dressed in chinos and a neatly-ironed pink shirt. He'd not thought it would be long before the stranger approached him, and it wasn't.

'Could you use any company?'

'I *was* beginning to feel a little bit lonely.'

'Let me get you a drink. Your glass looks to be empty.'

'Thanks. It's the house white. It's a bit el plonko but not bad.'

'I'm Carl.'

'Adam.'

The other moved through the crowds at the bar, men parting to let him through as if they sensed something about him that ensured they did that. That was what Adam had sensed too. Carl was middle height and very compact, with short brown hair, brown eyes, an aquiline nose, and a mouth that moved only slightly when he smiled. He had the look of a man who knew how to take good care of himself. Adam liked that, that impression of tightly coiled strength, even of danger. Not that Adam wanted himself involved in any kind of aggro, God no, but you could feel protected with someone like Carl at your side. And just occasionally, when the pubs were closing, you had to be careful if you were gay. He couldn't help a shudder even now when he remembered that night . . .

When Carl returned it wasn't with glasses of house white, but a full bottle of Chablis on a tray with two clean glasses. It was a wine Adam adored, with its delicate steely taste.

'Oh, Carl, it's not my birthday!'

The other gave his small smile. 'I had you figured as a boy who'd appreciate it.'

'I certainly do.'

They sat in one of the open-ended cubicles and Carl poured generous measures. He did everything with a sort of feline grace. Like an actor, he seemed not to make an unnecessary movement. He wore a seersucker shirt striped in two tones of blue, stone-coloured twill pants and soft brown-leather loafers. He'd laid a linen jacket at his side. Adam knew everything about the cost of clothes and could tell that Carl's were the best that money could buy. His eyes widened when his shirt cuff drew back on a gold Rolex that he could price to within £500 of ten grand. Adam was certain no one would attempt to snatch *that* from Carl's wrist when his cabriolet glided up to red lights in London. Adam bet he was right about the cabriolet too and about him living near London. He could tell by the accent.

'Lovely wine, Carl. Such a nice change. Are you in Bradford for long?'

'Just passing through. I have friends in the North-East. But they say there's some fine country round Bradford. Dales, moorland. I wouldn't mind spending a week or two to look round sometime.'

'Oh, it's *marvellous* country! Great coast-line too. Some of the villages, you'd think you were in the century before last.'

'I reckon I'd need a guide who had it all together,' the other said, giving Carl a meaningful glance.

Adam was beginning to feel very good and

it wasn't just the wine. This could be his lucky day. Someone like Carl as a boyfriend, tough, wealthy, obviously keen. It would give a whole new slant to his future. But he knew he mustn't get ahead of himself, knew he had to bear in mind that he might just be being chatted up for the night.

'What line are you in, Carl?'

'I spend a lot of time in Africa. I buy things, sell things.'

'And make quite a bit of profit going by that magnificent watch.'

Carl gave his little smile. 'I've managed to get a few bob to one side. How about you?'

'Oh, *boring*.' Adam pulled a face. 'Humdrum. I work at a Renault showroom and garage. Service reception. Says it all, doesn't it?'

'Nice motors, Renault. My old mum had a Renault Nineteen. Swore by it. They don't make them now.'

'That's true. We've just got one left. Use it as a courtesy car. Very reliable.'

They chatted on, Carl telling Adam something of the African countries he'd been to, sometimes touching Adam's arm in a way that gave him a little thrill. It was turning out to be a great evening. He hoped against hope they might be going to have a future. What if Carl lived in one of those gorgeous flats overlooking the Thames like Cilla and Michael Caine.

Outside, when the wine bar closed, Adam said, 'Where are you staying? Norfolk Gardens, I imagine.'

'Unless you've got a better idea.'

'I've got a flat along by Lister Park.'

They took a taxi. Adam's flat was one of several in a large converted mansion that had once belonged to a wool merchant when there'd still been a wool trade. Adam was rather pleased with his immaculate lounge, with its off-white suite and its tie-back curtains and its Edward Hopper prints, things he'd bought with a small legacy from his great-aunt Noreen. But when he'd closed the door and switched on wall-lights, and turned to Carl with a warm glance, his heart missed a beat.

Carl wasn't smiling, and when he didn't smile his face looked incredibly cold and hard. Adam began to tremble. It was what all gay men feared. He'd sensed that whiff of danger, but he'd not thought it was anything to do with him. He'd seemed to be such a decent bloke to those he took to. If people were into the other stuff they told you frankly, or the word got around. But Carl was a stranger . . .

His mouth was so dry he could barely

speak. 'I don't do rough-house, Carl,' he croaked. 'There are some who do, at the wine bar. You only had to ask.'

Carl seized him by the throat. It was like being caught in a metal clamp. Adam tried to speak, but all that came out was a terrified mew.

'Listen very, very carefully, Adam, and you'll not get hurt. I already knew you were in service reception at Jarvis and Co and that the firm has a Renault Nineteen. What I need to know is who was in the Nineteen yesterday when you loaned it out. The name, the address.'

He abruptly released his grip on his throat and Adam almost collapsed on to the sofa, holding his neck and trying to swallow.

'I don't intend to wait too long,' the other said. 'As you've gathered, I'm a busy man.'

Adam, his entire body shaking with fear, gave him a pleading glance. 'I don't . . . I don't know, Carl. I really don't *know*. We get so many people in first thing, waving keys at me.' His voice sounded as hoarse as if he was getting over a heavy cold.

'I've got ways of improving your memory. Don't tempt me to try any.'

'I just . . . I just can't remember. Please, Carl, you've got to believe me, got — '

The blow was like being hit by a brick. It

sent him sprawling from one side of the sofa to the other. He seemed to be looking through a haze of coloured rain at the man crouched over him like a wild animal ready to spring.

'Please don't hurt me any more, Carl,' he pleaded, in a whisper. 'Please don't hurt me any more.'

The pain and shock left him almost unable to think at all, but as the coloured rain began to clear he also saw his assailant held a thin-bladed knife. He barely felt the contact through the pain, but he knew he'd been cut. His face! His looks! He screamed, 'It's Crane! It's Frank Crane! Office on Manor Row! Don't *know* his home address. That's all I *know*!'

'That'll do nicely,' Carl said, slipping the knife into a sheath attached to his calf. 'You could have saved yourself a lot of aggro if you'd told me that at the start. Sorry we'll not be taking that holiday together, but as you've probably guessed I'm not a fucking shirt-lifter.'

★ ★ ★

Crane said, 'I have to know what's going on, Jane.'

She picked up the wine-glass with a hand

74

that still shook, drank what was left as if she needed it. Crane poured more from the bottle.

'You don't, Frank. Believe me. I should never have involved you in the mixed-up life I've got. I just had to find out about Dora.'

'I don't like any of this. Someone's trying to track you down and you're frightened.'

'Let it go,' she said, in a low voice, her troubled eyes moist in the half-light. 'Just let it go. Please. I told you before, I'm not in any real trouble, whatever it seems. Please believe me.'

'I can't. He might not seem to be trouble, whoever he is, but it doesn't take much to tip an obsessive over the edge. Men who've been kicked out who go back and kill the woman, maybe the kids. Well, you've read the papers. Believe me, I was once a police detective and I've seen it all.'

Her glance jerked on to his. 'This isn't a police *matter* — '

'It looks like one from where I'm sitting. I'm going to have to alert them if you won't explain.'

'You can't!' she suddenly cried. 'You *mustn't!*'

'Look . . . Jane . . . ' He put a hand over hers across the table. 'What if this bloke does track you down? Loses it? I couldn't live with that, because I'm the one who might have led him here. You've got to see the position I'm in. On top of that it could do my reputation a great deal of damage, if it got out.'

'You . . . can't . . . tell . . . the . . . police.' Each word was separately ground out between clenched teeth.

'I'd have to. I have no authority to do anything in my own right. I'm a jobbing PI.'

'If you do I'll tell them nothing. *Nothing.* It's my private *business*, not yours, not theirs, not anybody's.'

There was a look of near-panic in her eyes now that puzzled him even more. She seemed to fear police involvement as much as she feared the man who seemed determined to track her down.

'What if you got hurt?'

'I won't get hurt.'

'How can you possibly know? It's Dora's husband, isn't it? This Harry. He couldn't hack it, the way you and Dora were, so he legged it. And he sat in a furnished room and brooded about it. And now he either wants you back, or he's wanting to pay you out for wrecking his marriage.'

Her mouth fell open. You couldn't fake surprise and this was the real thing. She watched him for some time in silence. Then she gave her sad smile and shook her head.

'You couldn't be more wrong. You really couldn't. And that's why I want you to let it go.'

'If it isn't Harry out there then who is it?'

'I . . . can't tell you.'

'Can't, or won't?'

'Look, none of this would hurt your business, whatever happened. But nothing's going to happen.'

'My reputation comes a long way behind your safety. There's something seriously wrong in your life, Jane, there's got to be.'

'Frank — '

'Just tell me why you're stuck out here. You've no friends, I can tell. You lock yourself up like a caged animal. Why leave Woking in the first place; why — '

'For Christ's sake!' she suddenly cried. 'Don't start that police shit all over again. You did a job for me. You did it well. The rest is none of your business!'

'When you're so lonely and frightened and unhappy you're down to giving the hired help a meal? Well, the job's finished, but I'm doing this for free. It's because I care what happens to you.'

'Oh *God!* Will you leave me alone. Just leave me *alone.*' She burst into tears. Then she rushed out of the room. He heard her pound upstairs, the slamming of a door.

He poured himself more coffee, shook his head. He wondered what now. Maybe she was right. Maybe it was time to walk away, leave her to sort out her own complex affairs. So far he'd got none of it right, so maybe it was just too much for an outsider to get his head round. People lived funny lives.

Five minutes later she came quietly back. She'd dried her eyes and tweaked her make-up. She gave an impression of having thought things over. She gave him a calm resigned smile and sat down again. 'Bastard,' she said. 'You don't give in, do you? All right, I'll tell you how it is.'

He watched her for a short time in silence. 'You don't have to. Not if you really don't want to. I was out of line — '

'It was only because I didn't want to involve you in my messy life. Or anyone. I was out of line sending you to Woking. But well, the bond between Dora and me . . . It's not what you think, but you can't begin to know how strong it is.'

She sipped a little more of the wine. 'About three years ago my father became very ill. Then he died. We were shattered. He'd been a great dad to Oliver and me. My brother. And Mum, well, they'd been together since school-days . . . '

She watched him in a short silence,

swallowed. 'Mum was in a terrible state for months. But . . . but she met someone else in the end, through an amateur artists' society she was in. He was very kind to her, talked her through it all — '

She broke off, finished the wine, poured coffee from the jug. 'Well, a year later she married him. No one would ever replace Dad but she needed someone to lean on. I think he wanted . . . something else. Well, I know he did.'

She broke off, but Crane, who'd seen it all, knew what was coming. 'He had his eye on you?'

She fiddled absently with her coffee-spoon. 'Robert . . . Mum's new . . . he began coming on to me. It . . . well it really was like an obsession. Touching, stroking, trying to kiss me goodnight when I went to bed.'

'Your mum didn't twig?'

'He could make it come across as fatherly. You wouldn't believe. She never noticed a thing. She was happier than she'd been for a year just having a man around.'

She took a deep breath. 'He started meeting me leaving the office. Trying to get me to go for a drink, all that. One night I was in my room, getting ready to go out. I didn't know it but we were alone in the house, me and that . . . that piece of shit. He came in my

79

room. I was half-dressed, no . . . no bra or top. He tried to get hold of me.

'I gave him a knee in the nuts.' She began to redden with an old anger. 'Told him if he didn't back off I'd tell Mum. He just kept saying he was crazy about me. Hadn't wanted it, couldn't help himself, the usual crap. He said if I told Mum it would send her into a depressive illness.'

'Was that likely?'

She nodded wanly. 'After Dad died we worked with the doctor, Ollie and me, to phase her off the tranquilizers, get her to stay positive, move on. He said she'd be on a knife edge for a long time. I didn't know what to do, Frank. There seemed no way out. I knew what it was like to be fancied, but I'd never known anything like this. He couldn't take his eyes off me. He'd come looking for me in the pubs and clubs. Tell Mum he was working late. She believed him. He was good at business, made a lot of money, and he was very generous to her. And to be fair, he was very kind to her. Just like he'd always been really.'

It was painful for her to drag out those last grudging words. She'd been young to begin learning the complexities of life, that the man she hated and called a piece of shit could also be so well-regarded by others.

She went on, in the same low, hesitant voice, 'I told Ollie finally. Felt I had to. He's a well-made bloke, wanted to flatten him, he was so angry. But well, we went down the pub and talked it through. We both knew the arsehole had it right, Mum wouldn't be able to handle it. And . . . and I knew he'd never stop coming on to me if I stayed at home.'

'So you went to Woking?'

She sighed, nodded. 'Dad was born there. Gran and Grandad had lived there till they retired. It felt familiar, friendly. There was plenty of work, places to rent. I got a job right off, at the Halifax. Advising on financial products and so forth.' She gave him a ghost of a modest smile. 'I'm pretty good with people.'

He also smiled. 'I should think the looks helped too.'

'But, well, I had to give them an address at home. I'd been positive that if I moved right away that would be an end of it; he'd have to accept it. Only he didn't. He came to Woking. Said he couldn't live without me. Said I'd have to spend time with him or he'd tell Mum he was leaving her, to be with me. He said that if I'd agree to see him on a regular basis Mum would never know. Sleep with him, that was obviously part of the deal.'

She fell into another dispirited silence, her

eyes moving to his, then darting away.

'So you came north?'

She nodded. 'Mum's side came from Yorkshire. We'd had holidays in the Dales. It wasn't going to seem too strange. I keep in touch with Mum by phone. Haven't given her a number. I say I travel for the firm, never know where I'll be for long, best if I ring her. If I gave her a number and an address she'd only let him know it. He's no idea where I am.'

Crane sat back in his chair. So that was it. He thought about it for a few seconds. 'But he may have pinned you down to a town,' he said, in a musing tone.

Her amber eyes had a haunted look in the shadowy light. 'I'm in regular contact with my brother, too. He watches Robert like a hawk. Ollie will sort it, in the end.'

'What if Robert rocks the boat with your mum after all, if he can't get through to you?'

'That worried me at first. But Ollie can think things through. He said Robert would only ever *pretend* he was going to leave Mum if I didn't give him what he wants. If he *did* leave her he'd know it would put the lid on everything. You see, whatever happened to Mum he'd know I'd be out of the loop for good.'

Crane nodded slowly. Ollie did seem to

have a head on his shoulders. She poured what was left in the coffee jug, shrugged. 'That's why I'm here. In hiding. That's why I get scared he might track me down, but I'm not frightened of him. Not Robert. I . . . just couldn't bear to watch Mum go through what she went through when Dad died all over again.'

'How long do you think you'll have to live like this?'

She shrugged again. 'It'll sort itself out. Even Robert's got to see sense in the end. It's been a bad time, but it won't go on for ever.'

He nodded. 'I hope you're right.'

'Well, there it is. I'm sorry to have come across as such a mystery woman. That swine has a lot to answer for. Can I get you a drink? Lager, brandy . . . ?'

'I'd better not, with the driving. No car, no job. If you have a sparkling water . . . ?'

'I think I'll have the same. Wine is so thirst-making. Do you want to sit in a comfortable chair?'

It was dark now. She drew the curtains, went through to the kitchen. He heard the sounds of the dishwasher being unloaded, crockery stowed away.

He pulled a face. 'Nice try, Jane,' he muttered. He didn't buy it. He knew it was true, he'd seen genuine anger there about

83

Robert. He could even believe it had driven her to Woking, but gut instinct was telling him it had been one truth covering another. And it was the second truth that was causing the real damage. She lived in fear. All the time. And there was a fatalism there too; as if she knew something bad was going to happen: it was just a question of when.

Once again she'd told him nothing. She'd told him the Robert story to get him off her back about the real one. It didn't explain how he'd been picked up on in Woking. Trailed north by someone in a car registered to a Woking property company, who was sharp enough to ring Jarvis Motors as a pretend copper. And he couldn't believe any one would make the sacrifices she'd made because of a dodgy stepdad.

But he was going to have to let it go. For now. If he started pointing out the holes in the story it would upset her all over again. And she was right, he did sound like the police when he got going. He couldn't help it. Some people were born coppers.

She came back with fresh glasses, sparkling water in a litre bottle, its sides misting with condensation. She said, 'Do you not have a partner, Frank?'

'I had once. But life being the tricky sod it is it didn't work out. And you?'

'I had . . . once.' Her eyes were moist again, in the half-light. 'That didn't last either.'

He said, 'I live a funny old life. I work longer hours than when I was a cop. I'll not have a bullet-proof pension like cops who go the distance, so I need rainy-day money. It's not as if anyone *dies* now before they're eighty-five.'

He knew that now he was concealing one truth with another. Couldn't admit that he worked non-stop to mask the pain of old wounds that wouldn't heal.

'It must be a lonely life,' she said, in her low husky voice.

She'd know. He was certain there was no one in her life now apart from the people she worked with.

'You get used to it,' he said, 'in the end.'

She seemed to shrink into herself, seemed small and vulnerable, despite the weight-gain. He glanced at his watch. 'I'd better be moving. Tomorrow's due to start very early. Thanks again. Maybe you'd like to have a bite with me sometime. I cook quite well. I call it getting in touch with my feminine side.'

The smile almost reached her eyes. 'I'm beginning to think you just might have a feminine side, behind that armadillo exterior.'

'Don't let it get out, for Christ's sake.'

'I'd like to, sometime — come for a meal.'

Crane put on his jacket and she went with him along the hallway. He took one final glance at her pensive face. She put a hand out very slowly, almost reluctantly, and clasped his arm. 'Will you . . . stay with me?' she said, in a voice barely above a whisper.

He watched her in silence for a short time. 'Are you sure it's what you want?'

'I don't know. I think so. I hadn't thought about it till now. I don't know . . . '

Something about her confusion made it the most touching come-on Crane had known.

'Do you . . . not want to stay? No . . . no vibes?'

He took her hands. 'I'd like to stay very much, if that's what you want.'

She didn't speak again. She led him upstairs, drew curtains in the bedroom, turned on a single pink-shaded lamp. Like the dining-room it was furnished with unmatching pieces: an old bed with a dark-oak headboard, a heavy dressing-table with a swivel glass, a flimsy-looking modern wardrobe, a circular bedside table in bamboo.

'I'll use the *en-suite*,' she said, 'if you'll use the bathroom. It's at the end of the landing.'

He smiled, nodded, went off. She went in the *en-suite*, took off her make-up, cleaned her teeth, brushed her hair, automatically checking the roots for signs of her true colour. She wondered if he'd really believed her about Robert. Her troubled eyes looked back at her from the glass behind the hand-basin. Well, it had certainly all begun with Robert, at least that was true. If it hadn't been for him she'd not have left Ashford for Woking, not have met Dora, and through Dora . . .

She'd had to tell him something. Had to. To get him to stop banging on like the policeman he'd once been. He'd *seemed* convinced. But he was sharp as well as tough. When he began to think it through he'd probably realize it didn't hang together.

She sighed. She should never have sent him to Woking. Had she only been patient she'd have been able to get through to Dora in the end. But she'd had to, when the phone was simply never answered. Dora was all she'd got. And it wasn't as if she herself was in any real danger. They'd told her no way. It was scary, but she was sure she was safe. And if she wasn't, she wasn't. She'd just about had it up to here with worry, unhappiness, being so *lonely*. Maybe she'd be able to tell Frank soon, when she could really trust him not to involve his police contacts. It was probably a mistake asking him to stay. But she kept dreaming of having a man in her bed again.

87

How long had it been? She wasn't even going to work it out. She gave a sudden shudder, though it was a warm night.

She'd turned off the bedside lamp and was in bed when Crane padded across the bedroom. She was naked under the summer-weight duvet and there was even more soft warm flesh than there'd seemed when she was dressed. But he'd been a long time without a woman and the excess was fine with him.

They made love in silence. Didn't kiss. He'd heard it said more than once that women put a higher value on kissing than sex itself. But she grasped him tightly with strong arms. He knew it was comfort sex for her, just like the comfort food she was beginning to eat too much of. He was an old hand at comfort sex. The half-dozen women he'd slept with in the past few years had all been pining for the one who'd legged it, just as Jane was. They never seemed to cotton that he pined too. They thought missing blokes, he thought Vicky. She was the only one who'd ever mean anything, but she'd also legged it. And now and then he wanted to run his hands over a woman's body. He wanted to smell her scent and hear the sound of exploding breath, and remember how it had been with her. They were like stand-ins, him

88

and Jane. You could line up the lights on them and plot the moves, you could even involve them in some of the action. But the real stars were always somewhere else.

Later, she still didn't speak. But she laid a hand against his cheek. Not long after, she fell asleep. He was glad for her, hoped he'd made an adequate substitute for the man she endlessly fretted about. He hoped she'd wake up feeling a bit better about things. If it was possible.

5

'Who *are* you? What am I *doing* here? Where's Tony? What is this place?'

Crane leapt out of bed. The curtains had been drawn apart by about a foot, and she stood in the middle of the room in a band of sunlight. She was still naked and was shaking so hard she could have had a tropical fever. She looked terrified.

'Well, who *are* you? I've never seen you before. Is this your house? Why did you bring me here? Where's *Tony*?'

'Jane . . . ?' He shook his head, trying to get his mind going.

'*Jane!*' she cried. 'Why do you call me *Jane*? What are you trying to do to me? Did you drug me? Drug me, then rape me? That's it, isn't it, the rape drug. That's why I can't remember anything. You slimy, shitty bastard. Well, you'll not get away with it. I'll call the police, get myself tested. I'm not embarrassed. I'll do it now, before I've showered. I only need press this.'

She darted towards the bamboo bedside table and thrust it aside. Something was fixed to the wall behind where it stood. He'd seen one before, a number of times. It was a panic-button. It would be wired to the nearest police station or security firm. Or both.

'Don't press that!' he shouted. 'You're in no danger from me and never were.'

'You put something in my booze. You must have. But you'll not get away with it.'

She'd almost touched the button before he could knock her hand away. He took her by the arms and dragged her away from the wall. She began shaking herself like a madwoman and managed to tear her right arm free. She bunched her fist and hit him with all her force on the cheekbone. She was a strong woman and the blow rattled his teeth. He'd never punched a woman and he wasn't about to start now, but he slapped her face. Hard.

She stood very still then, a dazed look in her eyes. She watched him in silence for a good ten seconds. An eau-de-nil nightdress lay on the worn brown carpet like a gleaming pool of water. She picked it up, slipped it over her soft plump body, then sat down on the bed.

She finally spoke. 'I don't know what happened then; I don't know what happened to me . . . Frank. It is Frank, isn't it?' She watched him warily as if not entirely sure. 'I'm scared. I'm really scared. Everything

. . . well, it all seemed to go in a big black hole, everything that's happened since — '
She broke off. 'I couldn't get anything together, anything recent, right up to you slapping me. I don't know what's happening to me, Frank, and I'm really, really scared.'

He sat down with her, took her hand. 'You had a total black-out?'

'When . . . when I woke up everything that's happened since . . . since I left Surrey, it had just gone. I was somewhere in the past. Couldn't get any of this together: a strange bed, a strange house, a man I'd never seen before. I'm . . . I'm sorry. I didn't mean to lash out like that.'

'Has it happened before?'

She gazed at him with wide, frightened eyes, finally nodded. 'A few times. Same sort of thing. Waking up not knowing where I am. Hardly knowing *who* I am. But after a while it passes and I'm all right. It's . . . it's never been as bad as this.'

He pressed her hand. 'Just take it easy. I'll brew some tea. Do you need aspirin?'

She shook her head, still pale with shock, apart from the reddening patch on her cheek where he'd slapped her. He went downstairs in his underpants. He remembered something then. He'd been good at French at school, had never let it go. He bought *Paris Match* maybe once a month to keep his eye in. He'd read about a man who'd found himself on Tours railway station without money or ID, in good health, uninjured and thought to be in his thirties. He'd no idea who he was or where he'd come from. The police had named him Patrick X. The experts who'd examined him had been of one mind: his amnesia had been due to a profound psychological shock that he'd not been able to cope with, and his mind had closed down.

Maybe her mind was trying to do the same. Was that possible? Were the blank spells straws in the wind for a total memory loss? And maybe last night had somehow been the trigger for this new black-out. One she'd said had been the worst of all. She'd slept with him, but her mind had been on the one who'd done the runner, the one who must have been Tony. Then she'd slept well, maybe for the first time in weeks. And maybe woken up thinking she was still in the fun days. Before Robert. Before Tony had gone. Could that be anything like the truth? With total mental breakdown on the cards if she went on living with the endless fear, loneliness and anxiety?

He made tea for her in a small brown pot and black coffee for himself, carried the tray up to her bedroom. She was sitting exactly as he'd left her, staring into space. He poured tea, handed her the cup, sat down at her side again.

'Who's Tony, Jane?' he said quietly. 'Your boyfriend in Woking? Ashford?'

She gave him a single glance, her face contorted with a level of pain he'd not seen outside a hospital. She was shaking again, and then she began to cry. Messily, lengthily, moaning like a wounded animal. He put both arms round her, just held her for several long minutes. He knew then it hadn't been a simple matter of Tony just leaving her. Something must have happened to him. A fatal illness? A car-crash? A lethal punch-up outside one of those clubs she'd once used to go to?

She finally stopped crying. She felt under her pillow and located a handkerchief. She dried her eyes. Her face swollen and blotchy, she looked more childlike and vulnerable than ever.

'I'm sorry,' she said, in a wavery tone, 'you can do without all this.'

He glanced at her bedside clock. He had the usual day ahead of him, but it was only seven. 'Why don't you talk to me? You know I'll give you all the help I can.'

She watched him from bloodshot eyes, wiped a last tear from her chin with the back

of her hand. 'No one can help, Frank. It's
. . . it's got beyond that. I just have to live
with it. Like I always have.'

'All the same, I'm certain it would help you
to talk about it.'

'Oh, I've talked about it,' she said heavily.
'I've talked about it for hours.'

'With Dora?'

After a few seconds, she gave a small
reluctant nod.

'Jane, you blanked out your near past, but
you still knew there was a panic-button you
could press if you thought you were in
danger. How was that, do you think?'

She looked at the device now, as if seeing it
for the first time. 'I . . . I really don't know. It
was there when I moved in. It must have been
disconnected.'

'From the police station?'

She shrugged.

'You seemed to think it would work.'

She got up and moved slowly to the
window, drew the curtains fully open. There
was an inner curtain of ruched and patterned
net. It shimmered in the early sun and the
strong light defined her body in the
diaphanous nightdress. He thought, poor kid.
Why couldn't there have been a man her age
sitting where he was, a genuine partner,
admiring her ripe, sexy, back-lit body.

'Please don't ask me any more questions, Frank,' she said, in her low husky voice. 'There's so much I'd like to be able to tell you, but I can't. And the worst thing is, I can't tell you why I can't. But, however it seems, I'm not really in any danger. Please believe me. And I'd love to come to your place some time. At least I'll be able to do that. They can't — '

She broke off. Who were 'they'? he wanted to ask, but didn't. He knew she'd not tell him anyway. Her name wasn't Jane either, and he'd at least have liked to know what her real name was. But he knew she'd not tell him that either.

★ ★ ★

He got in his car. A dark-green Mondeo cruised slowly past, with two youngish well-dressed men inside. Two execs probably, picking up a third for an early meeting. Otherwise the estate made graveyards seem busy, as usual. He needed to call at home first for a change of linen. The moment he turned the key in the ignition the hands-free began to ring.

'Frank? Mike Beesley. You'd better get your fucking arse down here, pronto.' His tone was unusually curt.

'What's the problem, Mike?' he said uneasily. 'Can't you tell me over the phone?'

'No, it's something you've got to see. Christ, Frank, you're beginning to cause me serious trouble. Get yourself down here inside an hour, right?'

The phone went down. Very worried now, Crane drove home, changed, left a message on the office answerphone for Maggie to rejig his appointments, then gave it the hub-caps down to Jarvis Motors. There was a build-up of customers round the service reception desk as young Adam seemed to be missing, and the man standing in for him hadn't Adam's touch with the VDU.

Crane's arm was instantly seized by Beesley, who marched him without a word to his office. One of the walls was half-glazed so he could monitor the action on the showroom floor, but this morning a roller-blind had been drawn down on the window.

He saw now why Adam wasn't at his usual post. He was sitting on a chair in front of the desk. His left eye was almost closed by badly bruised and swollen flesh, and a thin wound like a deep nail-scratch ran from near his right eye almost to his chin. It had stopped bleeding now but must have bled badly to begin with. He looked up at Crane nervously.

'Sit down, Frank. Tell him, Adam,' Beesley

97

said shortly, going behind his desk to sit in his own chair. Crane sat on a visitor's chair, which he turned towards Adam's. Spirits hitting zero he didn't need to be told: it had to be the man from Woking.

'Does Mr Crane know about me?' Adam said, in a subdued tone.

'Adam's gay,' Beesley told him. 'He's never made a secret of it and he's never gone round blowing a trumpet about it. He's been with us since he left school; he's one of the best men I've got, and he can do without this bleeding carry-on.'

Beesley's face was blotchy-red with anger.

Crane, dispirited, said, 'What exactly happened, Adam?'

Adam told him about the previous night: the stranger, the expensive wine, the chat-up, the terrifying things that had happened at the flat. His hands shook as he relived it, his healthy colour wiped away by the pallor of a fear that lived on. At times he had difficulty getting the words out, especially when 'Carl' had suddenly turned into the hard vicious thug of the flat.

Crane, sickened, wondered what on earth he'd got himself into. She'd insisted there was nothing to worry about, she was in no real danger, and here was this poor sod with his face pulped like rotting fruit.

'I'm sorry, Mr Crane, I can't cope with rough-house,' Adam almost whispered. 'He was twice as strong as me, looked as if he worked out. I suppose that's what attracted . . .' The words dangled.

Crane gave him a sympathetic nod. He was a good-looking young bloke. He'd be as attractive to gay men as a pretty woman was to straight. And he'd be just as petrified about having his looks damaged.

'You gave him my name, Adam?'

'For Christ's *sake!*' Beesley broke out, 'what did you bloody *expect?*'

Crane held up a hand. 'Take it easy, Mike. I can see what he's gone through. I feel very bad about it, believe me. But I need it all, in Adam's words, so I can sort it out.'

'I had to, give him your name and the place where you have your office. I tried pretending I couldn't remember it, but he gave me this.'

'It was very brave of you, but you should have told him right away. I can handle whatever he thinks he's going to do with it,' Crane said quietly and with a confidence he didn't feel. 'The long nick on your face, he used a knife?'

Adam nodded, the whites of his eyes suddenly flaring like the eyes of a startled horse.

'Hold on, Frank,' Beesley said. He was very

99

upset about the young man's state, though he must already have heard the story. He poured coffee from a jug on a heated stand and added a tot of brandy to the plastic cup from a bottle in a desk drawer. 'Here, son, drink this,' he growled. Adam took it with a hand that still shook and sipped gratefully.

Crane was having his quota of frightened people this morning. It was getting to him. He could do without men who were handy around knives. Adam's wound had no more depth than a bad scratch, which showed great skill by the blade-artist. It was meant to give him the shock of his life but leave no lasting damage. Not physical anyway.

'Could you describe him in detail, Adam?'

Could he! It was a description that couldn't be faulted, but then it was a face and body he'd never forget.

'Any special features? Any scars of his own, say?'

Adam took another gulp of the laced coffee. 'I just caught the edge of a tattoo above his right wrist. Could have been a bird, I can't be sure. I think he saw me looking at it. He pulled his cuff down and I never saw it again.'

Crane concealed a sigh. A man with razor-edge reflexes, who could look after himself and knew how to handle a knife.

Who'd known every cunning dodge to use to get through to the man he'd trailed from Woking, including a little skilfully judged violence.

Beesley erupted again. 'Well, what are you going to do about it? It's all down to you, Frank, whichever way you slice it, and I don't need any more aggravation at this garage!'

Crane held up a hand again. 'I hear you, Mike. There'll be no more come-backs, that's guaranteed. The guy's got what he wants now, right, which is my name and workplace. Adam, I really can't begin to tell you how badly I feel about the trouble I've brought you. It's all down to a client I was working for, a young woman. This man seems to have found out I'm working for her and is trying to get to her through me.'

'Well, send for the police,' Beesley said bluntly. 'The mad sod needs nailing. It's got to be the arsehole who rang giving out he *was* police.'

Crane nodded reluctantly. They'd moved into a different league here. Adam had been assaulted and he had to be allowed to report it. It would bring Christ knew what complications, but he'd have to deal with them as they came along. But he wondered why Adam hadn't reported it at the time. The answer soon came.

'Mike . . . ' Adam said hesitantly, 'I'd just as soon not go to the police. They'll think it was just a couple of gays having a domestic. They'll think I was a dozy bugger for taking a total stranger home. Well, I was a dozy bugger. It'll only waste time and they'll do nothing in the end.'

Crane could go along with that. He'd been police himself once and they'd certainly want to know why he'd not reported it at the time it happened.

'No, you *must* go to the police, Adam,' Beesley insisted, 'with that class of nutter on the loose. It's not just about you, son, though God knows that's bad enough, but there's every chance it's putting Mr Crane in danger, and the woman he's working for.'

'I honestly don't want to involve the police, Mike,' he said unhappily. 'I suppose if Mr Crane feels I should . . . '

'I'd sooner try to sort it myself, Adam. You're right, the police would regard it as low priority. It's me who's in the loop now, not you, but I'll know the bugger when I see him and I'll be watching my back.'

Adam's glance took in Crane's strong frame. 'If you nail him give him a good kick in the bollocks for me, will you?'

Crane smiled wryly. He kept himself in shape, but he wasn't keen to mix it with a man who kept a shiv down his sock.

'Well, I think you're barmy, both of you,' Beesley said, glancing at his watch, 'but I really haven't the time to argue about it. Take a couple of days off, Adam, till your face clears up.'

'I'd rather get back to work. I've told them I slipped in the shower.' He smiled wanly. 'I once did and it didn't look much different.'

'Well, if you're sure,' Beesley said, relieved. 'If I have to leave that ape in charge of the service desk much longer I'll have the punters smashing the windows.'

Crane got up, also relieved. He took out a twenty. 'I'll say it again, Adam, how very sorry I am. Take this as a token and give yourself a night out when you feel up to it.'

The other's waxy face coloured slightly. 'No,' he said, 'you're all right, Mr Crane. I forgot to tell you: when he'd cleared off and I'd got myself together I found he'd left a fifty note on the table.'

★ ★ ★

Crane was pushed for time when he got to the small office he rented, but he wanted to run the rest of the Jane story past Maggie. He needed to warn her to be on the lookout for the man who called himself Carl, though

Carl now knew enough about Crane to come on to him direct.

He could also do with her input. She'd spent her working life around police departments doing secretarial work, and in retirement now worked part-time for him and a couple of other PIs. She may not have seen everything but she'd certainly typed it all up.

'Well,' she said briskly, 'I didn't think it was a good idea taking this job in the first place, but we'll let that go. Now this Carl: it really doesn't sound as if he can be the stepfather. So if he's not he could have been hired by the stepfather.'

'Can't be a PI,' Crane said. 'How could he possibly afford to have a PI permanently watching Dora's place? And PIs don't do violence. And they certainly don't leave fifty-pound notes around when they've found out what they needed to know.'

'A funny, braggy touch that,' Maggie said thoughtfully. 'I'm a hard man but I've got plenty of readies and a peculiar sense of honour.'

Crane's spirits were now well into the freezing zone. 'Fists, knives, a walletful of folding. You don't think we could be talking villains here?'

'Could we be talking anything else?'

'So what's his connection to a woman like

104

her? Respectable job, respectable life and so on.'

She watched him over the VDU of his third-hand computer system. 'Could have been a boyfriend.'

She was only spelling out what he'd not been able to face spelling out for himself. Gangster totty, could that possibly *be*? But he'd seen so much fear and misery. A mind that looked to be on the edge of switching off the lights. But he had to remember that Jane had once been blonde and bouncy. She'd lived the good times in lively pubs and clubs. And lively pubs and clubs attracted dodgy characters. And this Carl had looks and charm, as he'd had no problem oiling his way into Adam's flat.

He nodded, sighed. 'And maybe he got jealous when she wanted to end the affair.'

'Wouldn't leave her alone. Wouldn't take no for an answer. We've seen it all before, Frank, in our time with the force.'

'So she legs it because she can't take any more. Changes her name, dyes her hair, lives on Blackbird. But he picks up on me, God knows how, and now he's one step from pinning her down.' He shook his head. 'There's still too much I can't figure out. I'm convinced she wasn't lying about the stepfather, but I never believed it was down to him she came north.'

She said, 'Maybe she met the villain in Woking and didn't twig what he was till it was too late. That happens too.'

'Thing is, I'm certain she's frightened of him catching up with her, but she keeps insisting she's in no real danger. I can't get that together, not with what the bastard did to Adam.'

'But don't forget, career villains are often good lads about wives and girlfriends. They can work off their violence outside the house. Maybe he'd never harm her but refuses to let her go. And she's had enough.'

He moved to the window. His office was in a building in what was known as the Old Quarter. A cobbled street, one of the last in town, ran below. Crane's Megane was parked down there. He guessed a smooth operator like Carl would already have pinned it down. He wondered uneasily what his next move was going to be. Try and tail him to Jane's? He could forget it. He'd shaken him off once, he could do it again, no problem. So what other options were open to him?

'What will you do, Frank?'

'Wait and see. Not much else I can do.'

'Maybe you should let Ted know.'

'Adam doesn't want the police involved, and I don't honestly think I'm in much danger from Carl myself. I'm not an Adam. He had a good idea Adam would leave the police out of it, but he'd not know how I'd react, and he'd not want any trouble with the law either.'

*   *   *

He went about his routine business for the next couple of days, without incident. He checked his back full-time. He didn't contact Jane. And he eventually discovered the appalling truth. They'd not been inside a mile of it, Maggie and him. The only thing they'd got right was that there was some villain in there.

And *what* a villain!

6

Nick Gardner had rung, fresh from studying newspaper back-copies in Woking.

'Jesus, Nick,' Crane almost whispered, 'the *Brewers*!'

'She should never have involved you, Frank. Keep right out of it. You've got to, if you don't want really deep-shit trouble. From a swivelling fan.'

'The *Brewers* . . . .This Carl then — '

'Real name Lenny. They don't come any harder. He was in the Paras, for Christ's sake. After that, a mercenary in Africa. Back now looking after the shop.'

'That was in the papers too?'

'No. Just the trial and the background. But I only had to see one name to tie it to another. I asked around among various low-lifes. All reading the same script: he's out there looking. He's very, very clever. Sadistic with it. Likes to scare the living shit out of them first and then . . . '

Crane slumped in his chair. He was in his kitchen having a quick meal. 'I can't get my head round this . . . '

'Just let it go, Frank. He's a mean, vicious

bastard and he doesn't make many mistakes. I doubt you're in any danger yourself; he'll just be waiting now for you to lead him to her. Not that it'll do him much good, because *they'll* be ready and waiting too.'

'All right, Nick,' he said heavily. 'I wish I could sound grateful for a first-class job, but you've told me a sight more than I ever wanted to know.'

He put down the phone. Appetite gone, he pushed his plate aside. He thought Nick had it right: he himself was in no real danger. And neither was she, she had her own protection, which would be a lot more efficient than anything he could provide. Nick also had it right in warning him to back off.

But he didn't know that he could. He'd never seen such unhappiness, and now he knew why. And knew why her mind was throwing black-outs. He was the only one who could give her any kind of comfort. She'd had Dora once, but the pressure on Dora had given her mental problems of her own.

The phone rang again. 'Crane.'

'It's me, Frank,' she said quietly. 'I wondered if you'd come and have a drink with me, if you're not too busy.'

Crane took a breath. 'Look, Jane, right or wrong I felt I needed to do some research.

109

About you, Dora and Woking.'

After a long silence, all she said was, 'Oh.'

'Jarvis Motors was contacted by someone pretending to be police, and then a young chap who works in the service department at Jarvis was knocked about to make him give the name of who was driving the Nineteen the day I went to Woking.'

She gave a shocked gasp. He briefly told her about Adam. There was another lengthy silence. Then, in a voice he had to strain to hear, she said, 'This . . . research, how much did you find out?'

'All of it. Most of it was in the papers, anyway, at the time.'

The silence stretched so long this time that he had to break it himself. 'Jane?'

'So you'll not want to risk seeing me again. I . . . I can understand.'

'I told you I'd be there for you and I meant it, but you must see I'm the only link to you he's got.'

'But . . . but you'd know how to lose him if he followed you. And even if he did find out where I lived what could he *do*?'

It was a valid point. Crane kept losing track of that. What could he do, the way she was protected? He could see her at the other end of the line with her sad eyes, thinking that he'd been scared off too, the only friend she

110

seemed to have in the city.

'Please, Frank,' she said, in the same small voice. 'I've been so lonely. I can't begin to tell you what it's been like to have you around, someone I could really trust.'

He thought about it. 'Right,' he said, 'I'll be there in half an hour. But won't they want to know what's going on, your — ?'

'They'd go bananas,' she said flatly, 'about me involving you. They'd want me to move again. I couldn't go through that. And he'd find me. He'll not give up. No, I'll keep schtum. They have their methods; they'll know when he's around. They'll just be waiting for him to make his move.'

Crane thought he could understand now that note of near-fatalism he'd heard once or twice before in her husky voice. He drove to Blackbird on a circuitous route. He pulled in to lay-bys. He back-tracked. He drove round the houses. When he finally rang her door-bell he was quite certain he'd not been followed.

But that began to bug him too. Why had there been no *attempt* to shadow him? How could he possibly make any further progress in getting through to her without following him? Not that it mattered if he did, he had to remind himself. Uneasily.

★ ★ ★

'I'm so glad to see you.' She put her arms round him, her amber eyes moist again. That tricky bastard called life had dealt her just about the worst hand it could put together.

She took him in the usual room, with its backdrop of woodland and rising terrain. There was gin on the little table, with mixers and ice; this time they sat together on the old sofa. It had been a cool day of low cloud and a single radiant of the gas fire hissed again.

'I'm sorry,' she said, 'really sorry. Using you like I did. It wasn't on.'

'It was because of Dora. I can see it all now. She daren't ring you and you could only ring her on a protected line. But they must have seen me coming here, right from the start. What did you tell them?'

'I said you'd called in at the office for advice on a Life policy and we'd got on. I'd invited you for a drink. They were satisfied . . . once they'd checked you out.'

He smiled wryly. He spent his life checking people out, didn't much care for being a checkee. He said, 'I suppose Dora's trouble . . . ?'

'She couldn't take any more. Poor darling Dora.' Her eyes glistened in the half-light. 'He was all she'd got, an only child. She tried so hard to come to terms with it. They both did, but Harry couldn't cope at all. That's why he left home. He hated me, *hated* me. He thought if Tony had never met me he'd still be alive. Maybe he would.' She brushed her eyes with the back of a hand.

'It takes people so differently,' she went on, in the thin wavery tone he'd heard before. She swallowed, breathed in, began again more calmly. 'Dora trying to live a normal life till her nerves gave out. Harry laying all the blame on me and leaving home. And me . . . well, you know what happened to me. Waking up with chunks of my life in a black hole.'

'Robert, your brother. They do exist?'

'Oh, yes.' She forced a faint smile. 'That was true, if nothing else. Robert did try it on and Oliver and me did think it best if I moved away. So . . . Woking, getting on with Dora, being invited home for a meal and . . . and then meeting Tony.'

Her eyes left his and she gazed without focus towards the darkening garden, her face expressionless. He put a hand over one of hers. 'Don't go on if it upsets you. I know the story. I can fill in most of the blanks.'

'He was a lovely man,' she whispered. 'You'd have liked him. Everyone did. He was always so cheerful, so full of life. Big, strong. The minute we saw each other, that was it.'

She sipped some of her gin and tonic. She

wore her usual subdued clothes: a grey T-shirt in jersey crepe above a long grey skirt. But the night she'd met Tony she'd have worn bright clothes, clothes that went with her exuberant blonde hair, and she'd have been thinner and vibrating with life, eyes shining.

'Dora was so *pleased*. We'd become such good friends and sooner or later we'd be related. Nothing could have worked out better.'

She began swallowing again, but he knew she wanted to tell him all of it. He guessed she'd wanted to tell him for days. Maybe it would be a good thing, to let it all out again, after the long months of enforced silence. Bottling it up could have triggered the black-outs.

'We . . . we were hardly ever apart. Three months later we . . . we moved in together. Rented a flat in Roundthorn Park. Christ, I wish we'd never gone near the place. It gave me bad vibes from the start. It was near a lake and that spooked the shit out of me as it was, don't ask me why. I thought it was just the lake . . . '

She ran a quivering hand through her hair. Her entire life ruined by a single incident, all this suffering, and none of it her doing.

'Brewer . . . the father: Donny — he owned quite a few houses and flats on the estate, buy-to-lets . . . well, you probably know. There were a lot of people like me and Tony: young, on the move, needing to be handy for London. Tony worked a lot in London, fixing computers on the blink. We shared the rent. Aimed to get married when we had a down-payment on our own place.'

Crane said, 'You knew Brewer owned your flat?'

She nodded, sipped more of her drink. 'Everyone knew about the Brewers, but he worked through managing agents. Charged fair rents too. It was all completely kosher.'

'Somewhere to channel the racket money?'

She nodded wanly. 'They could never hang anything on him. He laundered it too well, worked through too many iffy legal people. And kept himself out of any trouble, until . . . well . . . ' She looked away.

'My London contact told me Donny had been gradually phasing out of the rackets for a few years and into legal setups. He was getting too old for the rough stuff and starting to think of retirement.'

'The central heating had broken down!' she said, on a sudden high note. 'Can you *believe* it, a stupid silly thing like that? We couldn't get anyone to fix it ourselves. It was a lease condition that the agents saw to it. Something to do with making sure it was serviced regularly and didn't become dangerous. Anyway, the agents kept saying they'd see to it, but nothing was happening. It was autumn and the nights were getting cold. I feel the cold badly. I know I nattered on about it . . . '

He caught that haunted look in her eyes again, as if her nattering on could possibly have made her partly to blame for what had happened. 'It was the only heating we had, apart from a little bar-thing we'd borrowed from Dora. In the end Tony rang the agents and told them they had two choices: they either let him get someone in himself to fix it, invoice to them, or he suspended the direct debit for the rent, which was just about due. They wouldn't agree to that so he suspended the debit. The agents must have told Brewer's people. It was so stupid!' she cried. 'So bloody *stupid*!'

She gave a sudden sob. Crane took her hand. 'Take it easy. Here, let me top you up.'

He mixed her a stiff one and a small one for himself. He'd not be stopping tonight. Sex, even comfort sex, didn't go with the grief she was putting herself through.

'I'm sure it's just what you wanted,' she said thickly, 'some woman in a state after your hard day's work.'

'It's what friends are for.'

'It's not *me*, Frank, all this. You can't

116

believe the woman I used to be.'

'I think I can, you know.'

She sipped some of the fresh drink. If she had a few drinks and talked herself out there was a chance she'd be so drained she'd get a decent night's sleep.

'Brewer came round with some of his people,' she went on, as if compelled. 'Nothing to do with Tony stopping the debit: Brewer didn't get into that kind of detail. It came out later he was looking over another house he was thinking of buying. But he knew about the debit and I don't think he wanted to lose any goodwill. Tony was outside, pottering about. I saw Brewer leave the men he was with and come over. I knew it must be him, stocky but small, sharp suit. I honestly think he wasn't looking for trouble. He was smiling to begin with, keen to sort it, I think . . . '

She broke off, sipped more gin. 'Tony . . . he was a laid-back type on the whole, but he had a very short fuse when people were incompetent. He'd had it up to here with the cold flat and me belly-aching and the agents making excuses. I was inside but I could see he was having a right old go at Brewer. I *knew* it wasn't the way to talk to a man like him. But Tony . . . well, he could be hot-headed; he was a big guy, stood head and shoulders over him.

'Brewer . . . he'd gone red. I really believe he was trying to keep his cool. But everyone knew about his short fuse. He was the one who kicked arses. But Tony, he'd got carried away. They were shouting the odds now, and then Tony said he could stick his tenancy agreement up his backside, and the . . . Oh God! He shouted that the next place he rented wouldn't be from any fucking short-arse of a fucking *gangster*!'

She grasped Crane's arm, closed her eyes, back in the Roundthorn flat on that hazy autumn afternoon, the men shouting, the tall one stooped over the small one. And then those few fatal words that had made the knife suddenly flash in the small man's hand. And then in seconds the blood spurting on Tony's T-shirt like great flowers, and the total shock in his face, and the flash, flash, flash of the knife, and the insane satisfaction in Brewer's face when his pale eyes met hers.

'Tony couldn't believe it was happening. With him being so big and Brewer so small. He couldn't get near him. The second he saw the knife he lashed out but Brewer just dodged out of the way, and then he stabbed him, over and over again. He was dead in minutes, Frank, minutes!'

She began to cry again. He just held her.

He'd seen it all in the police: the bodies laid around car-crashes, the domestics, the closing-time punch-ups. You had to switch off, like a doctor, or you couldn't handle it. The dark patches came later, over a drink, the child still clutching its Snoopy, the newly-weds with confetti still in their hair, the graduates, high on their degree successes. Poor kid. Not just sudden, senseless slaughter, but the way they'd changed her from the bright, bubbly blonde she'd been into the sad woman she was now. The one who ate too much and whose eyes never lit up and who was condemned to living in silence on this silent estate.

She finally drew away and straightened up. Dried her face. Took a gulp of the gin. Her face was swollen again, and blotchy, but she'd cried herself out.

'Well, that's how it was,' she said, in a calmer tone. 'They bundled Brewer in the car and took off.'

'And he legged it.'

'He was on a private jet that same afternoon.' She sighed, gazed into the glow of the fire. 'It was the last thing he'd wanted, the police knew from their snouts, not in a million years. He'd done all that in East London, the heavy stuff, giving people a kicking in a pub lav. They reckon he only

119

carried the knife as a souvenir. He was middle-aged, wanting to wind down, legal businesses. But ... well, he just had this crazy, uncontrollable *streak*. It scared the shit out of the people who knew him. That's how he'd got on, everyone was so scared of what he could do if he lost it. They told me, the police, that everyone in the Brewers' world knew you never, ever, ever mentioned his height. He'd once killed a man in a pub lav for saying more or less what Tony said.'

'Did no one see it? The Roundthorn Park people?'

'They were mostly like us, out earning a living. Tony and me were just having a day off. If anyone did see, they didn't let on.'

'Tell me about it,' Crane said bitterly, who couldn't begin to count the number of cases that hadn't made it to a courtroom because of people not letting on.

'They'd flown Brewer to Spain,' she went on, in her low husky voice. 'One of the detectives told me, off the record, if it had been a gangland killing they'd not have wasted much time on it, but this was an innocent member of the public. They pulled out every stop there was: task-force, man-power, snout, the whole bag of tricks. Well, they nailed him, hiding out in a villa in the hills behind the coast. Beard, tan, shades, lifts in his shoes. But the Spanish extradited him. And that was it except for the trial.'

'And you the star witness.'

'The only witness,' she said, in a near-whisper.

'Why did they put you in the Witness Protection Programme?'

'They . . . they said they had no choice. MI5 told them they'd picked up vibes that Brewer's son, Lenny, had said he was going to see to me for grassing up Donny. They said he was worse than Donny. Cunning. Twisted. Very controlled. He's wanted for all manner of things they know he's done but can't pin on him.'

She shuddered again, then broke out in a sudden harsh note, 'I wish I'd never gone near any courtroom either. It couldn't bring Tony back and it's ruined my life. And Dora's. She feels threatened too. The police have warned her to be careful. No set routines. Vary her routes when she drives anywhere — in case they try to get to me through her. That's why she had to go in the Brookfield. Not just her son being murdered, as if that wasn't enough for anyone, but all the aggro since. We've ended up in a worse state than the Brewers. Oh *God*, Frank, they've taken everything, my bloke, my life, my confidence. I can't do *anything*. I might just as well be in prison, like Donny. At least he's had company.'

He took her hand again. 'It won't go on forever. They'll get Lenny. Sooner or later they'll make something stick, and then you'll be able to live a normal life again.'

He knew neither of them believed it. If they'd not managed to nail Lenny after all this time they weren't going to. He said, 'What about your own people? Your mum, Oliver . . . ?'

'They know I'm in the programme, but not where I'm living. They can write, but the letters take ages to get through the system. They can't phone. I can phone them, on a supervised line, so I don't let the slightest hint drop of where I am. That's why I couldn't find out what had happened to Dora. I could contact her but she couldn't contact me. I could have asked the police to find out, I suppose, but they get so edgy about things like that. They don't really like me being in touch with *anyone*. It's costing them so much as it is, in time and money, guarding me, keeping me in a safe house . . . ' She shrugged. 'They try their best, I know that, but I always end up feeling I'm just being an expensive nuisance!'

'They brought you north to be well away from it all.'

'They've got a special arrangement with the Leeds police. Not Bradford. They want to keep it completely under wraps, even from the force of the town I'm living in, apart from a handful of people at the top.'

Crane glanced at her. As levels of risk went they weren't graded much higher. 'The morning after the night I stayed, I saw a car drive by with a couple of youngish blokes in. I thought they were business types. Surveillance?'

She nodded wearily. She looked to be all in. 'Cars come and go, park here, park there, so as not to get the neighbours going. I never know where they are, but I always know they're somewhere around. They told me not to even think about it, just to get on with my life as normally as possible. I should be so bleeding lucky.'

She sighed. 'I had to dye my hair brown after the trial. I'm really a natural blonde beneath the colour, believe it or not.'

'Is that so?' Crane said, as if he'd not known since day one.

'When I go out I wear glasses with plain lenses, awful clothes, drive a really boring-looking car.' She glanced at the clothes she wore tonight, pulled a face. 'I never used to own any clothes like these. I liked bright things, especially when we were going down the boozer.'

Her life had been changed out of all recognition. She could have been a woman in old age, living alone, partner and friends dead and gone, going through the motions of living like a sleep-walker, till she died too. With death maybe coming as a blessed release. Maybe that was how she'd come to see herself. It would explain the near-fatalism.

He said, 'Look, I'll stay with you if you want me to, but I think it might be best if I don't. Just tonight.'

She nodded. Understood. She'd been able to talk it all out again and she was totally drained. He knew she'd sleep now. But staying with her, she'd almost certainly turn him into Tony again. And then maybe wake up with an amnesia even more frightening than the last.

'Please stay in touch, Frank. You've been so good for me.'

He pressed her hand. 'I'll call by most nights, even if it's only for half an hour. And we've got a date at my place, don't forget. Maybe Saturday. Your real name's Colette Jennings, right. Do I call you Colette now?'

'I'd love that,' she said wistfully. 'But only when we're alone. I've got to be Jane everywhere else.'

'You'll have a completely new ID? Driving

licence, bank account, Social Security number . . . ?'

She nodded. 'Sometimes I think I *am* Jane Kennedy. Maybe I'll have forgotten her altogether one day, the blonde who went clubbing in red T-shirts and pedal-pushers and drank Bacardi Breezers. Gossiped in the bogs and never went home till chucking-out time. The one who met a bloke who was so much what she wanted she could hardly get her head round it.'

They were some of the saddest words Crane had heard, and he'd heard plenty. She blinked several times, but the tears didn't gather. The tear-ducts seemed to have dried up from over-use.

She saw him to the door, kissed him warmly just to the side of his lips. 'You'll ring me tomorrow, won't you? Even if you can't come round?'

He nodded, went down the drive in the darkness. He'd heard the locks being engaged and the soft whirr of the intruder alarm being set, but he felt suddenly wary. It was the old police instinct from the days when he'd had a lot to be wary about. It was a wariness that began to turn to tension, as if something was going to happen, even though Brewer couldn't possibly have pinned down the safe house. And what if he had? A car was parked about ten yards away, so everything looked to be in order. A pair of experienced DCs on one of their endless spells of guard duty, poor sods.

When he'd driven on to her road, Crane had swung his car round in the cul-de-sac area so that he'd be parked in the right direction for moving off later. He got in, keyed the ignition, switched on the head-lamps. The police detectives' car faced his, and Crane's lamps lit up the windscreen. The car looked to be deserted. Maybe the man, or possibly woman, had ducked out of sight. Crane couldn't shake the impression some-thing was wrong. What if there was no one in the car? But it was unlikely they'd leave it unattended on this kind of operation. One of them should be in the car, watching the front of the house, and one somewhere in the back garden covering the rear. They'd spell each other, half an hour at the back, half an hour in the car with the thermos.

He put his foot to the clutch, slid the lever into first. Then he drew it back to neutral, turned off the ignition. There had to be something wrong. He was certain there was no one in the car. He got out, began to walk towards it, in the total silence that blanketed Blackbird Common.

As he drew closer his heart lurched. He

could see that the pavement side door hung open by a couple of inches. The man inside lay with his legs in the well of the steering-wheel, the upper part of his body slumped across the passenger seat. He was either unconscious or dead, his face a bloody mask from the blows he'd taken, the lapels of his jacket soaked in blood. Crane opened the door fully. It disturbed the body, the arm of which slid sideways, the hand dropping with a thud to the floor of the car.

Crane stared bleakly down. He'd done it, Christ knew how, the murderer's son. Found the house he'd been searching for with such dedication and expertise.

And where was he now?

7

Lenny relaxed over a drink, smiled his thin smile. A good night's work. It reminded him of the African days, when you'd fight in any war and on any side that paid the most. He'd got to be so good they'd always sent him in ahead of the rest. There'd be young blacks guarding whichever village they were knocking over, ready to raise the alarm, but they never got to raise the alarm because Lenny would slither silently up to each one, a few inches at a time, clutch them by the throat so they couldn't get a sound out, let them have the knife between the ribs and into the heart. No one could do it better than Lenny, that single thrust to the heart. The smile became nostalgic. They'd been great days.

Not that he'd killed the police guys. Pity, but kill a pig and you never saw an end to the heat and hassle. He'd just roughed them up a bit. No one had his touch either for knowing exactly how far to go. They'd not be a pretty sight for a week or two but they'd get over it. The thing was, it would scare the living shit out of Colette fucking Jennings.

Bitch! He could have got in the house and

whacked her on the spot, the minute the PI had left. Locks, intruder alarms, do me a favour. But he wasn't going to whack her, was he, not just yet? He was going to make the bitch suffer. He smiled again, took another swig of his lager. He'd not lose touch with her now, and when he'd scared her so much she daren't even put her nose out the door, *that's* when he'd whack her. The pigs had taken her from the place on Blackbird Common, but he knew where. They were no match for a man with his training, who had the powerful infra-red bins and could hide himself behind a garden shrub, and could run like an antelope with a lion up its arse.

She'd pay. For putting the old man in Belmarsh. Just when the poor old guy was talking about putting his feet up after all those slogging hard years in the rackets. He'd been thinking about cruises, a nice villa on the Med. Would you believe, one of the first places him and Ma had wanted to go was *Africa*! Not to kill any blacks, just to go on safari and see the elephants and the giraffes. Ma'd been mad to see the animals, and now she'd never see them, because when the old man had done his bird they'd be past it, even if they were still alive.

Lenny stared into space, a brooding look in his dark eyes. No, she had to pay. She should never have shacked up with that big dozy arsehole in the first place, snivelling on about the heating and then calling the old man a short-arse. The old *man*! Gordon *Bennett*! Didn't he know what had happened to Bertie Fox in the piss-hole at the Bucket and Bow, for fuck's sake? No, he was one of those stupid sods didn't know shit. So he gets the old man to lose his temper and now the old man was in Belmarsh because the totty couldn't keep her big flapping mouth shut. It was *all* down to that great clown of a boyfriend; so why couldn't she just have kept her head down and then they could all have put it behind them and moved on? Didn't she think he hadn't enough on his plate trying to look after the business without having to take time out to see to her? *Bitch*!

His face had become hard and angry, but he knew it got him stirred up whenever he thought about the crappy deal the old man had had. He had to keep his feelings out of it, play the cool dude like he'd done in Africa, and do an efficient job. He began to think about the PI. That always made him smile. He must be doing his nut. How had Lenny Brewer tailed him from Woking? How had Lenny Brewer pinned the totty's house down? He was never going to know. But he was pretty sharp, all the same. He'd managed to shake him off on the Ml, hadn't he, to some tune. But no one was sharp enough to beat Lenny in the end. He'd been born working out the angles.

★　★　★

'We need to talk, Frank,' Benson said. 'Can you be in the Toll Gate over lunch?'

When Crane got there, Benson, wreathed in smoke as usual, led him to the quiet end of the bar. 'Look,' he said, 'this goes no further, but this woman you did that job for on Blackbird, two plain-clothes men were given a right going over outside her place last night. I was wondering if it was anything to do with the bloke who followed you that time. She didn't let anything slip, by any chance?'

Crane had spent half an hour trying to decide the best way to put this. 'Look, Ted, I know all about it. They were Leeds police and they were on obbo at her house. She's in the Witness Protection Programme.'

Benson reddened. He obviously wasn't in the loop. 'Well, I knew they were from Leeds, but how the fuck do *you* know all this?'

'I've . . . been seeing her. Her real name's Colette Jennings. Her partner was the bloke Donny Brewer totalled, yes?'

'Colette Jennings . . . ? He had her placed

in part of a second. 'Colette Jennings! I thought she was from the south. Holy mother! So who did for the DCs? And why were they Leeds people, for Christ's sake?'

'It's got to be Lenny Brewer, Donny's son. Or one of his people. The Woking police wanted Leeds to handle it, even though Blackbird Common's in Bradford.'

Crane had rarely seen Benson so angry. He jabbed out one cigarette, reached for another. He guessed it was partly because he'd not been trusted with the information by people further up the line, partly because Crane knew everything about it and he knew nothing. It reminded him too much of the old times, when Crane had been police too, and they'd worked together on so many cases.

'Look, Ted,' he said evenly, 'you know how it is with the WPP. They regarded Lenny Brewer as ultra-high risk because he's one very skilled villain. So they put Colette in one town and guarded her by police from another otherwise things can get out, you know they can. We also know that here and there are bent cops who can be encouraged to let things slip.'

'Well, it hasn't fucking worked, has it? They give it to Leeds and they blow it.'

'With Brewer they're up against one of the hardest men around. He was a Para and then a mercenary in African war zones.'

Benson watched him, still seeching. Then he said grudgingly, 'Well, seeing as you have the inside track, what exactly happened last night? I suppose she told you.'

'I was there, Ted. I'd gone for a drink with her. I'd been cleared to visit. That's when it all came out, about her being Tony Powell's girlfriend. About being the only witness to put Donny inside. She's had the hell of a life since. Anyway, I left lateish, found one DC beaten up in his car. The other DC was in the back garden, also half-dead. I got Colette to open up again. She's got a direct line to the Leeds police. There were two cars and an ambulance there in minutes. They'd have been Bradford police, yes?'

The other nodded dourly. 'No explanation. Just two police from another area needing urgent back-up.'

'Two other cars came not long after,' Crane went on. 'They were from Leeds. Told her to pack a bag and go with them. Told me more or less to sod off, not to ask questions, and to keep my trap shut.'

'And you only found out she was in the WPP yesterday?' Benson said.

He sounded suspicious. Crane felt a twinge of guilt. Maybe he should have told Benson about the belting Adam had had. But Adam had insisted the police were kept out of it, and at that stage Crane and Maggie were still wondering if 'Carl' might have been some rough-trade boyfriend Colette had got herself mixed up with.

'Yes,' he said, 'I only knew the real story yesterday.'

'She's been a bloody fool,' Benson said, 'sending you down there.'

'She knows it.'

'She knew you were tailed from Woking. Why didn't she tell them then?'

'Because they'd have gone berserk about her employing me.'

'Stupid bitch.'

'Hold on. The only friend she had was Dora Powell, and then Dora wasn't answering the phone. So Colette cut through all the bureaucratic crap and set me on. How could she possibly think Brewer would be able to pick up on it? Christ, how *did* he pick up on it?'

'She should have gone through her minders. They must have told her a hundred times what the form is.'

'Now look,' Crane said tersely, 'all right, the kid made a bad mistake. But her head's all over the place, believe it. She can't see her family or her friends, and that lot in Leeds don't even like her seeing *me*. She might as well be in solitary and she knows it. And all because she stood up and said, yes, that arsehole in the dock's the one who slaughtered my boyfriend over sod-all. Use some fucking *imagination*!'

'I am doing,' the other snapped. 'She's got two choices: does she want to live like she has to live, or would she sooner be dead?'

'It's a good question and she's having such a crap existence I think death's getting to be an option, unless you can think of anything in particular she's got to live for.'

They were both flushed now. 'Yes, well,' Benson said, 'two young coppers took a battering for Colette Jennings. How are the rest going to feel when it's their turn for guard duty?'

After a silence, Crane nodded, his old police instincts aroused. They'd taken a hell of a beating, and if he'd still been in the force he knew he'd be thinking exactly as Benson was. They both calmed down. Benson also could sense the way Crane's mind was split, half on his side, half on hers. He said, after a silence, 'How could Brewer have got a fix on the house, Frank?'

'You tell me. The one thing I do know is that he couldn't have tailed me. Not even with an accomplice in a separate car.'

'He couldn't have got in your office?'

135

'No problem to a man as sharp as him. Except that all client details are on the computer. You can't get in without a password. Only me and Maggie know it.'

'You say he's sharp.' The other lit yet another cigarette. 'But if he's such a sharp cookie why smash up two DCs? He must know nothing gets the police going like having their own killed or injured.'

'Oh, he knows. But he needed to make a point. They say he's a sadistic bastard, likes his victims to sweat first. I reckon he could have seen her off last night. But he just wanted her to know he'd been around, so he duffs up two plain-clothes men and legs it. For the time being.'

'So what's his next move?'

Crane sighed. 'I don't know, Ted. He must know they'll bury her somewhere else now, and this time they'll be watching her blink. So how does he stay in touch then? I don't know. I just know he fucking will . . .'

★ ★ ★

'Close the door, Ted. What's on your mind?'

'Colette Jennings. That's what the mess on Blackbird Common was all about, yes? I should have known, Terry.'

136

Jones, a heavy, greying man with deceptively mild features, gave him the steady, poker-faced look that had always been a valuable part of his stock-in-trade. 'How do you know now, Ted?' he said quietly.

Benson told him how Colette had hired Crane to go to Woking, how it had led to what had happened to the two Leeds DCs.

'Crane can't figure how Brewer could have got through to her, and neither can I. But I should have known, Terry, and if I'd known none of this would have happened. It was me who put Crane on to her in the first place, for what was supposed to be a routine mis-per.'

Jones nodded. 'Need-to-know stopped at inspector level, Ted. And this time with incredible emphasis, believe me.'

'Oh, come *on*, we all know about need-to-know, but you could have told *me*. You know it would have gone no further.'

Jones got up, went to the window, looked out over the city buildings, sharply defined in the clear afternoon sunlight. The features, trained to show no emotion in however difficult the circumstances, concealed a mind badly thrown. Benson was right, it could have been avoided, the trouble on Blackbird, had Benson been told. And they all knew about orders and rules and need-to-know. You bent the rules for people you could trust like you trusted yourself. He'd have trusted Frank Crane, trusted him with his life. Christ, he wished he was back! He could also trust Benson. But Benson had never been in the same class as Crane. And that business about Crane having to leave. Well, no one would ever know for certain, but as far as Jones was concerned the wrong man had had to go. Which was the main reason why he'd not tell Benson shit.

'I'm sorry, Ted,' he said blandly, turning back from the window. 'Normally, I could have filled you in on it, but the orders this time were written in stone. I'm beginning to see why. Tell me, is Frank romantically involved?'

'What do you think?' the other said sourly. 'You know what women are like around him. Can't see the come-on myself.'

Neither could Jones. The man had such nondescript looks: tall, well made, forget the face. And about as much smooth talk as a bin-man. But women took to him. He'd heard that one of the young WPCs had been found crying in the toilets when Crane had been given the welly.

'Well,' he said, 'they'll bury Colette Jennings this time like she was nuclear waste. I doubt he'll ever see her again.'

'So long as Brewer doesn't,' Benson said,

still brooding about the original grievance. He also knew that if Crane had still been in the force *he'd* have known about Colette Jennings. That sod had always known *every-fucking-thing*.

★ ★ ★

She knew she should have been trembling with fear; instead, she was just angry, very, very angry. Seething. It was anger, not fear, that had kept her awake much of the night. How much longer did she have to creep round like this, like a mouse? Colette Jennings, bubbly blonde, always up for a night on the town, always enjoying life, screaming with laughter. And now spending her life creeping round like a *mouse*!

Well, she knew how long it would go on like this. For good, that was how long. Because how old was Brewer? Mid-thirties? About Frank's age? He'd *never* give in. And the police were like three men who knew sod-all. They were supposed to be guarding her, for Christ's sake! Only Brewer had made mincemeat of them, it had been so easy. He'd found out where she lived, and if they took her off to China he'd find her again. So what was the point? What was the bloody *point*?

She'd slept a little in the end, but when she awoke she still felt exactly the same. It was over. And never again. She'd left her back on Blackbird Common, the poor cow who fastened a dozen locks on the door every time she came home. Who brought work from the office to pass the time, who cooked meals big enough for an elephant because food and booze was all there was when you never saw anyone and never had sex and never went to the boozer or the clubs. And look what it had done to her figure! You could count her ribs at one time, in the days when her belly went in instead of out and Tony could get his hands to meet round her waist.

Well, it was all over, little miss scared of her shadow, whose memory kept going down the plug-hole. She smiled briefly. She owed so much to Frank. God, to have met a real bloke, who didn't piss about with the smooth talk, but whom you could absolutely trust and believe in. They'd insist she dropped him now, and then they'd want to cart her off to a new safe house. Well, they could get stuffed, on both counts.

Someone knocked. Showered and dressed, she opened the door. One of the police detectives stood there, holding a breakfast tray. 'I got you this Colette. It's continental. I didn't think you'd want the great British fry-up.' He smiled faintly. 'I'm Dave, by the way, and a DS.'

'Thanks, Dave. You were dead right about the breakfast. I need to be at my office in Bradford for nine. Can you arrange that?'

He gave her a startled glance. 'I . . . don't think we can do that. I think the idea is to find you a new safe house.'

'Yes, well, today I'm going to the office and I'd like transport.'

The policeman's face hardened slightly. 'Look, you must know it's completely out of the question. We're talking Lenny Brewer here — '

'Christ, I've been *thinking* Lenny fucking Brewer since they put his old man in Belmarsh. I know all about Lenny Brewer and I need to go to my office!'

'You can't be serious — '

'Try me.'

He watched her, confused, then handed her the tray. 'I'll be back.'

But he wasn't. Instead, an older man knocked. He was weighty with a pink healthy face, a large pulpy nose and brown hair just on the turn. He was neatly dressed in a dark-blue suit and striped tie.

'Miss Jennings . . . Colette, could I have a word? I'm Inspector Burton.'

141

He came in and gave her an avuncular smile. 'DS Skelton tells me you're asking to go to your office. Colette, surely you must know that's out of the question.'

'Not to me it isn't. I suddenly decided during the night that I'm not going to go on living like a rat in a cellar. I'm going to my office today and if your people won't take me I'll ask reception to get me a taxi.'

'Look, Colette,' he said gently, warm smile still in place, 'I know it's been a dreadful experience for you, but I must ask you to do exactly what we've arranged. For your own safety. We can't be sure, with a man like Brewer, that our people weren't followed here. Take my word, he'll not follow us to your new safe house. You'll be going there by helicopter.'

'Then you'd better make it tomorrow because I'm going to the office today. They've been good to me and I want to hand over the clients I'm dealing with and warn them I'll need time off for an emergency.'

'We can take care of all that. We've handled these situations before. All you have to do is take a helicopter ride, and by evening we'll have you in a decent new billet.'

'No,' she said, 'and I'm not prepared to argue about it. I don't have to do anything I don't want to do, and I'm going to the office.'

'I don't think you need take quite that tone — '

'I take the tone that gets me through to people. You were supposed to be *guarding* me, but you made a right old pig's arse of that, yes? Well, Lenny Brewer would find me again if you hid me in a coal-mine. So I might as well go to the office, because it makes no difference whether he gets me now or later.'

'Now look here!' he suddenly barked. 'Two of my men sustained horrific injuries last night guarding you, and I think the very least you can do is co-operate with us for your own safety.'

'And you look here,' she cried, 'I said I wasn't prepared to fucking *argue* about it!'

They stared at each other angrily. Burton couldn't get it together. Colette Jennings was supposed to be a quiet, amenable type of woman, badly traumatized by the killing, ready to co-operate and accept that the police knew best in cases like this. But the woman he was trying to deal with was coming across like a back-street tom.

Colette suddenly picked up the bedside phone, keyed zero. 'Reception?'

'Put it down,' Burton said quickly, 'and leave it with me.'

★ ★ ★

The car's hands-free rang. 'Crane.'

'It's . . . me.'

'Where *are* you?'

'At the office.'

'After what *happened*!'

'I insisted on coming in. Wouldn't take no for an answer. Shouted at them.'

There was a steely edge to her husky voice he'd not heard before.

'Where did they take you?'

'Queen Hotel. They fixed it so I by-passed reception. Two of them stayed with me in a connecting room. They tried to make me take off with them today for another safe house. Another town, another job, dyeing my hair ginger. Well, the jury's still out.'

'What does that mean?'

'Listen, I'm speaking on my mobile in the office bogs. If I suddenly clear someone's come in. But I'll keep in touch.'

'So when do you leave? Tomorrow?'

'Goodbye,' she said abruptly. The line went dead.

Crane drove on. He couldn't work that out, the police letting her go back to work. She'd insisted, she said, had shouted at them. It didn't sound like the grieving woman on Blackbird who'd fingered a killer and now lived in a state of permanent fear. None of it made sense. He'd been certain they'd have spirited her away at first light. But she'd shouted at them. And they'd backed off. She was within her rights to do as she liked, but it seemed bloody odd.

His mind picked at this for most of the afternoon. Then he began to wonder if the police might just have an agenda of their own. Had backed down in the end because it might be to their advantage. If Brewer had got it together on where she'd been living, maybe he also knew where she worked by now. And maybe the police had thought there'd be a good chance he'd be watching her office building, once he'd picked up on the fact that they'd let her go in today. And maybe they thought they'd have a good chance of nailing him. They'd have accurate descriptions of him from the southern police, if not any actual mug-shots, assuming he'd always managed to stay ahead of the law. If they could nail him today they could charge and remand him, for the damage to the two DCs. Then sort out Colette's new safe house tomorrow, knowing they didn't forever have to keep looking over their shoulder.

Could that be the plan? As an ex-cop he knew it had to be worth a shot. Colette now as apparent bait, two or three unmarked cars, half a dozen of their finest, watching every other car in the area. Checking every male who opened a car door, or walked near the office building, or went inside. If that was the plan he hoped they'd now really grasped the nature of the beast. Crane had known few villains with Brewer's mixture of skill, ruthlessness and cunning.

His mobile rang in the late afternoon, when he was checking and signing the post Maggie had left for him.

'It's me again. Where are you?'

'In the office.'

'Have you a fax?'

'Yes.' He gave her the number. 'What is it?'

'I need to send you something. And tell you I'm taking off.'

'For a new safe house?'

'No,' she said shortly. 'Taking off on my own.'

'What's that supposed to mean?'

'What it says. I'm going off, on my own, to lead my own life.'

'Are you right in the bloody head?'

'The fax is coming through. I'll ring back when you've seen it.'

She cut off abruptly, as before. Seconds later the fax began to whine. He was glad Maggie wasn't around. The first sheet was a facsimile of a flash photo of the man Crane had found badly injured last night. It showed him exactly as he'd seen him, slumped across the front seat of the unmarked police car, his face and jacket lapels covered in blood. Bleak-faced, he watched the second sheet inch its way out. It was a copy of another photo, taken against undergrowth and showing a second man with his face pulped, and lying on the ground. That would be the DC who'd watched the house from the back garden. A third sheet edged its way out of the machine. He didn't spook easily, but this threw him. It was a copy of a hotel façade. It was the façade of the Queen.

His mobile rang again. 'He's saying he knows where they took me last night and where I am today.' He'd expected the words to come unevenly through trembling lips, but he was wrong.

He said, 'Where did the fax come from?'

'The agency on Market Street. You can pay to send faxes and e-mails if you haven't got your own gear.'

'How could he know someone else in your office wouldn't pick up the sheets?'

'He rang. Asked for me. Said he was faxing some information from Friends Provident that Mr Shaw wanted urgently,' she said, in the same hard-edged tone. 'He even knows the people I work with. Friends Provident, we're in touch with them a dozen times a day, so it all seemed pukka.'

'What did he sound like?'

'Well spoken. Sounded like one of the men we do actually deal with at FP.'

The sod could do passable impressions too. A Guildford policeman for Beesley, a well-bred exec for Colette.

'Colette, you've *got* to pass this stuff to the police. Why haven't you?'

'Because they're useless. He could have *killed* me last night, if he'd wanted to. He didn't do it then because the sick, shitty bastard wants me to suffer first.'

She'd worked it out for herself, only too accurately.

'They'll have a whole raft of police on it now. It'll have top priority. It's not just you, you know, it's the DCs who bought it.'

'They can do as they like, Frank, my mind's made up. Those faxes were the last straw. I'm taking off.'

'Don't talk bollocks. You'd not have a cat's chance on your own. The police wouldn't let you go. They'll not want you out of their sight now, after last night.'

'I'm getting out,' she said flatly. 'Don't you see, the more the police crowd round me the better for him to know where I am. So I'm going to go off quietly on my own. I'll find somewhere to live and I'll get another job and I'll mix with people again, like a human being.'

'Colette,' he said, in the calmest voice he could put on, 'you're not seeing straight. You know he'd catch up with you in two minutes without your minders.'

'The thing is, Frank, guess what, I don't care. At least I'll be able to live what life I've got left normally. I just don't *care* about Brewer. Can't you see, whether the police bury me again or I live my own life he'll still get me? So I might just as well live my own life while I can.'

'You're just playing silly buggers. The police'll not let you go anywhere unguarded.'

'Don't think I've not thought it through. They'll not know I've gone and neither will he.'

'Get real. And don't even think about a disguise. Dark glasses, a hat, a different jacket, do me a favour. It'll not make a scrap of difference, the way they'll be watching.'

There was a brief silence, then she spoke in a warmer tone. 'I've got to go, Frank. It's been great knowing you, really great. I'm so sorry I've given you all this grief. I'll be in touch one day.'

'You're *certifiable*! It *is* a disguise, isn't it?'

'I've got to go. Time's running out.'

Crane, agitated, began to pace up and down his little office. 'You might get past the police, but you'll not fool Brewer. Even if you do, how long before he twigs? Minutes. You'd never make it to the station, you'd not even get out of the Old Quarter.'

'I've had enough, Frank. You've seen how I was living.'

'Don't do it. You know what he's capable of — '

'I'm going to have to cut you off — '

'Look, I'll pick you up. At least that way — '

'Oh, no, Frank, no, no, *no*! That's how it all started, because I involved you.'

'You'd not get as far as Cheapside. I don't care how well got up you are.'

She was silent for a few seconds. Then she said quietly, 'No, Frank, you've done too much for me already.'

'Let me at least get you clear of the city. I can lose anyone who tries to follow. I can get you to a station. There'll be half-a-dozen police outside your office and a nut-case and you need *help*!'

Another silence. Then, 'I just didn't want to give you any more aggravation,' she said, her husky voice almost a whisper.

'I'll be waiting in Vicar Lane, yes? What time?' he said, glancing at his watch.

'Sixish. That's if . . . if you really won't take no for an answer.'

Crane left a note for Maggie, telling her to reschedule any calls he'd arranged for tomorrow. Tomorrow was Saturday, but just another working day for him. Maggie only dropped in for a short time, on her way to the supermarket, to deal with any urgent calls on the answerphone.

Then he rang Jeremy Green, a solicitor he'd done a fair amount of work for in the past couple of years. They got on well.

'Jeremy, Frank Crane. Your little place at Gargrave. If you're not using it yourself this weekend could I beg the loan?'

'We're not and it's yours. You can't be taking two whole days off!'

Crane chuckled. Fat chance. 'Could I call for the keys now?'

'You can. There's food in the freezer, including bread, and milk and eggs are a minute's walk away on the high street.'

'Thanks a lot, Jeremy. I owe you one.'

By five to six he was parked in Vicar Lane, the keys to the holiday place in his pocket, the address in his diary. It was his till Monday, not that he'd need it for more than one night. He just needed to get the stupid bitch to some quiet place where he could sit her down and talk some sense into her. It was risky, but nothing like as risky as letting her go it alone.

He carefully scanned the street. They were all office buildings now, the tall, graceful wool warehouses of the fifties and sixties. He thought of the steely note he'd kept hearing in her voice. It couldn't have made a bigger contrast to the way she'd sounded at the nondescript house on Blackbird. He'd seemed to be talking to a different woman. Or maybe it was like talking to the woman she'd once been, who'd loved life and laughter and putting her best togs on. She'd had enough, she said, and sounded as if she meant it. She didn't care any more, and sounded as if she meant that too. He shook his head. But Benson had it right: did she want to live like she had to live, or did she want to be dead?

Time moved on. It was five past six now and no disguised Colette walking towards him. Maybe they'd spotted her. If so, they'd be furious, especially if they were still hoping Brewer was going to make some kind of move. They'd think she'd ruined the entire operation.

The rush to get out of the city was almost over, but a group of men and women in business clothes strolled down Vicar Lane, talking and laughing, with the air of people heading for sundowners at the Glass-house. One of the women was blonde and giggly, and made Crane think of Colette as she must once have been: the week's work done, a couple of quick ones with her workmates and a weekend of non-stop fun to look forward to.

Still no Colette herself. 'Fuck it,' he muttered. If she'd been intercepted she'd probably not even be able to phone him. It could be months before he saw her again. If ever. By half-past six he'd have to assume the worst. Or the best, depending where you were sitting.

The group of chatting strollers drew near his car. Through the open window, he heard the blonde woman say, 'I'll catch you up, guys. I just need to touch base with my boss.'

'OK, Polly, see you . . . '

They glanced round to smile at Crane through the window, and then the blonde woman opened the passenger door and slid in at his side.

'I regret having to say it, miss,' he said, 'but I think you've got in the wrong car.'

'Good,' she said. 'If it's fooled you it has to have fooled them.'

'*Colette!*'

8

Lenny waited patiently in his souped-up, maroon Ford Focus. He was wearing a woman's wig of honey-coloured hair and his face was carefully made up: lipstick, powder, blusher, eye-shadow, false lashes. He wore a padded bra beneath a fuchsia T-shirt, which had a flower-print on the front of mock rhinestones, and blue, stone-wash denims. He even wore a pair of women's sandals because Lenny became agitated unless every detail was absolutely accurate, not just what folks could see.

He knew the disguise worked. He'd driven round the area twice to get the lie of the land, and the pigs in their unmarked cars hadn't given him a second glance because they weren't looking for a woman. And now he was parked diagonally opposite the entrance to the office building, looking as if waiting for a boyfriend, and nursing a silenced pistol. When she came through the door, and he had a good clear shot; he'd poke the gun just over the window-sill and let her have it. As there'd be no distinguishing sound it would look to the pigs as if she'd tripped and fallen, and Lenny, as the nice inoffensive little woman, whose engine was already idling, would drive off casually, one car among several.

It was high risk, but it was carefully calculated, and he'd taken plenty of them in the past. He could handle it. And he had to see to her today because they'd be taking her to a new safe house tonight, and if they were right in the head they'd be flying her there. And it would give Lenny a lot of grief to track her down again. It was a pity it had to be right now as he'd hoped to get a lot more fun out of scaring her knickers off. But at least he'd sent her the three faxes to make sure she was having a really crappy day.

But Lenny's powerful instincts were beginning to warn him that something was wrong. He could tell the pigs sensed it too. He could see one of the police cars through his rearview and he'd clocked heads being shaken at the way things were going. The building had to be empty now; it was Friday, for Christ's sake, and nearly 6.15. Since that bunch of women and suits there'd been no one else. And she'd not been among them. He knew what she looked like now, or what they'd got her to look like, and there'd been no one who'd looked like that. Not that he could have made with the hardware had she been among them, that would have been a risk too far.

Lenny stowed away the pistol in the glove compartment, thinking hard. He was becoming certain she was no longer in the building. If they were waiting to fly her off to some other part of the country what point was there in her working late in a place she was never going to see again? It made no sense. And if she wasn't in the building she must somehow have got out of it. It was an old building, tarted up, and he knew there was no other exit. So if she'd got out she must somehow have disguised herself. Why? Why would she want to give her pig-minders the slip? He wondered if it could be something to do with the gum-shoe, Crane. She'd been with him last night. Maybe he was giving her one. And maybe she wanted him to give her one last one before they dragged her off from Bradford for good. It seemed a stupid thing to do, but women were stupid, especially when they had the hots.

It was all guesswork, but Lenny had lived his life by guesswork when he was in central Africa. And he'd got it right more than he'd got it wrong. He gave his thin little smile, glad now he'd not whacked her tonight if there was the chance of a bit more fun. So, if he'd got it right, he'd better concentrate on the gum-shoe again. 'For my next trick, ladies and gentlemen . . . ' he muttered, the smile widening slightly.

★   ★   ★

Crane gave it the hub-caps along the by-pass route. It had been a mixed summer day of ragged cloud, showers and hot sun, but the sky had cleared now. They passed farmland and scattered hamlets. Tree shadow was lengthening and the ridges of distant hills showed purple in the declining light.

Again, he knew he'd not been followed. He'd checked his back at every stage. Neither of them had seen the same car twice, with Colette watching as intently as him through the passenger-door mirror.

'The wig,' he said.

'Bought it a long time ago. To remind me what colour my hair really is. I'd sometimes wear it in the house.'

'You packed it last *night*? With all the hassle?'

'I'd not dream of leaving it behind.'

'And the clothes?'

'Kept them in my office locker. Told myself that one day I'd change into them and really go to the Tavern, or the Glass-house in local parlance. Never dared to though.'

She sounded almost cheerful. Maybe she felt more like she'd once used to be, with the bright clothes and the makeover. The blonde wig was shoulder-length and wavy, and she'd used blusher and a bright lipstick. She'd done something with eye-liner that had given her eyes almost an almond effect, and attached diamanté ear-rings, She wore a dark-red blazer over a white slash-neck top, and a shortish check skirt. She'd given herself a dab of a slightly musky scent. Crane was still very uneasy but had to admit it was brilliant. He'd not thought she'd be able to do anything with her appearance that would really fool the police. He hadn't thought she'd go for totally in your face: vibrant, colourful, the girl who stood out in a crowd.

She must look now as she'd looked in the carefree days of her freedom, and would the police, or Brewer, believe she'd take such a high-voltage risk? They hadn't and it had worked. A double bluff.

'How did you cotton on to those people?'

'I got lucky. When I went in the lift they were coming down from the top floor. Insurance brokers. I did the big smile, said I was a new girl on the block, and could they recommend a decent pub for a drink and a snack. They said come on board, they were all going to the Glass-house.'

She was grinning. He'd never seen her grin. Just smile, sadly. Maybe she'd managed to put it on ice, the difficult life she'd had to lead, the endless loneliness and fear. There were actresses who could do that, he'd read, briefly lose their real selves in another character.

She said, 'I can hardly believe it, being able to pull the blokes. Even though I'm getting these bloody love handles and haven't done dolling up in months.'

He wondered if the sexy saunter and the giggly manner had been thought out with the same care, or if they'd suddenly come naturally as soon as she'd begun to look like the scented swinger she'd once been. 'You took a hell of a risk,' he said. 'You couldn't have stood out more if you'd been wearing a polka-dot bikini.'

'They were looking for a dowdy mouse with glasses and dark hair,' she said, with sudden contempt for her old, subdued alter ego.

'We'll have to let them know you've taken off,' he said, 'the police. They'll be running around like headless chickens.'

'I'll ring them. Where are we going anyway? I thought we were making for a station.'

'I thought we'd let things cool down. Tomorrow, I'll take you to Leeds station, or Wakefield, and we'll slip you on a train that's heading where you've decided to go. Meanwhile, we're going to a village called Gargrave.'

He cleared a roundabout and began to drive along a road that gave a view of the first soaring fells of the Dales, and an impression of a wider sky. She gazed out hungrily at the pattern of glowing fields, the motionless cattle, the blurring horizons, the occasional flash of water.

'You know, Frank, I had a marvellous life till . . . till Brewer killed Tony. My brother Oliver, he was a great pal, we always seemed to be outdoors: tennis, cycling, swimming, playing with the other kids. And then, when it started with the blokes and the parties, and being able to make decent money, I had just as much fun. These past months, I've often wondered if maybe I was *too* happy. Maybe they decided I'd been given too much happiness in one go and now they had to level it all out.'

The words touched Crane where he felt it. He put a hand briefly over hers. 'They'll get him, Colette. Now they know he's around. And once they do they'll tie his DNA to the beatings he gave the DCs. They'll have gone over their jackets with special equipment. It only needs a hair these days, or a flake of skin.'

But the words sounded hollow to his own ears. The best chance they'd had for nailing him had to have been today, but she'd blown it for them by taking off.

Shortly afterwards they reached Gargrave. It seemed little changed since the days when Crane had motored through with his parents on the way to holidays in the Lakes. The same bridge over the river, the same railings along the bank, the same little rain-shelter, the same tranquil high street. It gave him a stab of nostalgia. Because his life had been happy too, until the happiness had ended as abruptly as hers.

Jeremy's place was a terraced cottage on the green. Crane parked in front of it. The house was probably Edwardian or even earlier, and had casement windows and a chimney and roses climbing the brickwork round the solid oak door. It had been extensively modernized inside. There were chintzes and a flowered fire-screen and Windsor chairs and a gate-leg table. But there was also central heating and double-glazing and a state-of-the-art television and DVD-player, concealed in a cabinet with cabriole legs.

There were two downstairs rooms, the big living-room that opened from a tiny hallway, and a small dining-kitchen. The kitchen had all the gear too, behind rosewood panels: cooker, micro, washer, dish-washer, fridge-freezer. A central table would seat six, and a lattice window overlooked a rear garden, with laburnums, flowered borders, a small lawn and neat hedges. The river would run beyond it.

'Tony would have loved this,' she said, looking out into the gathering dusk. 'He was very ambitious. We'd buy our own starter home and then move to a bigger house and have a couple of kids, and then we'd buy a weekend place, in Dorset or South Devon. He knew he'd make it. He was already being head-hunted for a big selling position because of his skills and his gift of the gab. He loved his work. He loved life. Like me.'

He glanced at her but she was in control. She could barely mention his name before without crying. She was different. He'd sensed it the second she'd slid into his car on Vicar Lane. It wasn't just the wig and the clothes. It seemed to him as if her real self had broken through the protective skin of that sad, withdrawn woman he'd known before. This is who I really am and it's time to move on.

Except that she couldn't move on. And soon Crane was going to have to tell her to forget it. It wasn't going to be easy, not with the new Colette. He pressed a switch. It turned on wall-lamps and a concealed strip-light over the food-preparation area.

'Christ, I'm hungry!' she said. 'Wouldn't say no to a drink either.'

He smiled faintly. Her appetite was intact at least. Or maybe it was a carry-over from the long lonely months, when it must have seemed that food and drink was the only way to fill the emptiness.

He opened the freezer. 'Take your pick.'

She sorted carefully through the contents. 'How about steak and kidney pie?'

'Whatever you say.'

'Maybe a game-soup starter and apple-pie and ice cream for dessert. And there's some Brie too and a French stick. Great stuff . . . '

He left her to it, knowing he was probably going to be given twice the amount he normally ate. He'd leave a cheque for Jeremy to cover the cost.

She slipped out of the blazer and began to study the cooker controls. He searched for booze. There was plenty of it in one of the elegant cupboards. They both wanted gin and there was a lemon in the fruit bowl. He wondered whether to open a bottle of wine to have with the food. Maybe they still needed to keep their wits about them, even in this peaceful spot. Though he didn't see how they could possibly have been traced, no one had even begun to twig that the chatty blonde had that morning been a brunette in glasses. Yet Brewer had this incredible knack for pinning her down.

He took out a bottle of Chilean Merlot. The food and wine would relax her. Get her in a receptive mood for the tough talking he'd need to do later. When she'd sorted out the cooker, she picked up her gin and tonic with a sigh of pleasure. 'Give the grub forty-five minutes.'

He thought what a hell of a day the kid had had. Probably hadn't slept much last night either. Then a shouting match with the police to force them into letting her go to work. Then the fax churning out horror pictures in what should have been the safety of the office. Telling her he knew exactly where she'd spent the night. Brewer was good. Bloody good. Mercenary-soldier good. How could police detectives, who couldn't be expected to have his kind of intensive training, be expected to match his expertise? It depressed him.

'Well, that's it with the programme,' she said. 'I'm all right for money. If you never go out you never spend any. I'll find work, a place to live.'

'We'll talk it through when we've eaten,' he said. She didn't pick up on his neutral tone.

164

He was convinced this was the real Colette. Animated, positive, she was near-hyper with the excitement of fooling the police and leaving her half-life behind her.

She ran a hand affectionately over the cap of gleaming blonde hair. 'You can't believe what it feels like. Sitting in the kitchen with the dinner cooking, with a *bloke*. We used to do it such a lot, me and Tone, when we weren't going out.'

'You'll do it again, one day. You're young, resilient, you'll meet someone else.'

'You're probably right. There'll never be another Tony so I'll not be trying to find one.'

It made sense. She'd want kids, a home, a man about the place. Most women did. And she'd know how to share herself, between the new man and the man she'd never forget, so that the new man didn't get jealous about any ghosts.

'I'll pay you back one day, for all you've done for me,' she said.

'Forget it.'

'I don't forget things. Not the way you've been. Shall we try another gin?'

He still couldn't get used to it, this intense, almost desperate eagerness for life. She spotted a radio and tuned it to a music station. She wanted to chatter, about nothing in particular, the words almost merging, her scarlet lips a blur of movement. It looked to Crane as if she was trying to make up for the lost small talk of the long silent months in half an hour. She got him to talk too, though it was not something Crane normally ever did, about his own youth and the crowd he'd gone about with, the moorland hikes, the booze-ups, the trips to the coast in an old banger.

It was difficult to believe she'd been so close to death last night. She was burying it beneath stories of her Kentish girlhood, giggling so much at times she could hardly get the words out. She told him about a fancy dress party she'd gone to in a bear costume. The head was plastic and too big, and kept falling off. When it was on she couldn't see properly and kept walking into furniture. It had fallen off again when she'd been standing at an open upstairs window and had hit a man on the head who'd come to pick up his daughter. Then the man's dog had seized it and run off into woodland. They'd organized a tipsy search party, but the head was never recovered. It was the way she told it, and Crane began to see what great company she must have been, and how popular. In the end, Crane was laughing openly, something very rare for him.

And then they heard the chiming of the front-door bell.

9

They stopped laughing. 'Christ,' she whispered, 'no one knows we're here.'

He put up a warning hand, turned off the radio, moved silently into the living-room and then into the little hall. He'd hoped there'd be a viewing-glass but there wasn't. As he stood there, trying to decide what to do, someone knocked. Maybe they thought the door-bell was out of action. It was more a tentative tap than a knock.

The door was on a chain at least. He opened it a crack. It was dark now, but there was just enough light to see that it was an elderly man. Relieved, he slipped the chain and opened the door fully.

'Oh, good evening, sir. Do forgive me. I thought it must be Mr and Mrs Green. I'm Tom. Tom Bower. I keep an eye on the cottage when Mr Green's away. Let the meter-folk in and so forth.'

Crane had turned on the hall-lamp and could see that he was stooped, grey-haired and smiling diffidently from behind wire-rimmed glasses. He wore baggy flannels, a wrinkled check shirt and a cardigan whose

167

buttons were fastened one out of synch all the way down. Crane sensed Colette move into the hallway behind him.

'We're friends of the Greens. He's lent us the cottage for the weekend.'

'Of course, sir, of course. Do forgive me for intruding. As I say, I usually call round to see if Mr Green needs anything. Milk or eggs, that type of thing. Would *you* like anything, sir? I only live next door.'

'We're just sorting ourselves out, Tom, and I'm not sure what we'll need yet. Perhaps in the morning . . . '

'Of course, sir, of course. The house to your left.'

'That's very kind of you.'

'I do hope you enjoy your stay. There's good walking, if you like walking. There's a particularly nice walk along by the viaduct. You cross the bridge and turn right.'

'Thanks a lot, Tom, I know the area pretty well. We'll see you in the morning.'

He closed the door, slowly but firmly. 'This is how it goes in the country. If I'd not shut him up he'd still be out there at ten o'clock.'

But the chiming bell had broken the mood. Its unexpectedness had given them both a shock. Reminded them of the people they really were, and what they were doing. On the run from both the police and Lenny Brewer.

The food was ready and they sat down to eat. First the game soup and the crusty bread, and then she divided the pie into two large helpings. Spooned on the mixed vegetable. She glanced at him self-consciously. 'I've got to stop eating like this. I will, once I'm back in the real world. I only began to eat too much when . . . ' She let the sentence dangle, then burst out, 'I got so fucking *bored*!'

He nodded. He knew. He poured some of the Merlot into plain goblets. She sipped some, watching him over her glass. She said, 'I once knew a reformed alcoholic. He said he could always spot other reformed alcoholics. They all showed signs he could identify with. Same with me. I can always spot real deep-down sadness in someone because I've spent so much of my life being a sad sack myself. What's your story, Frank?'

'You don't want to know,' he said. 'Believe me.'

'It might make you feel better, to talk about it.'

'It wouldn't.'

'It did me. To be able to let it all out to you. It hit the black-outs on the head. For good, I hope.'

'I don't get black-outs.'

He sometimes wished he did. Could wake up one day with a completely fresh sheet, like

169

that Patrick X in Tours.

'You know so much about me. I know nothing about you. Except I know you're a good bloke behind the hard-bitten attitude.'

Maybe it was the wine. Maybe it was the way they'd been thrown together. Maybe some of her vulnerability had rubbed off. 'There was this villain,' he said suddenly. 'He was the most evil piece of human garbage I'd ever known. Drugs, prostitution, illegal immigrants, protection, you name it, he did it all. And the way he protected himself no one was ever going to nail him, unless someone fixed some evidence. So me and my colleague fixed some. We'd had it up to here with young women, bits of kids, with their jaws broken, and crack skeletons, and Asians with their shops torched. Only this arsehole had the best legal team money could buy. One of them spotted the fix. So I put my hand up, the case collapsed and that was the end of my police career. The villain ended up with a bullet in his head, but that's another story.'

'Oh, Frank,' she said softly. 'And your colleague as well, I suppose — '

'He has a wife, kids. His wife is in poor health. If he'd lost his job he'd have been in really deep-shit trouble. There's not a lot open to a man who's been kicked out of the police. I was living on sod-all for a long time before I turned the corner with the agency. But I was single, had no responsibilities. It was either me putting my hand up for the lot, or both of us losing our jobs. That made no sense.'

'He must have been very, very grateful. Was it the man who gave me your name, right at the start?'

Crane drank some wine, sighed, his eyes unfocused in the half-light. 'My mum once told me you should only do someone a favour if they were in a position to return it one day. She said if they couldn't return it they'd never forgive you.'

She put a hand over his, across the table. 'Frank . . . '

'We were best mates, not just colleagues. But since then . . . ' He shrugged. 'Not even the friendship really made it. Sometimes I get the impression that he's trying to convince himself that *all* the dodgy stuff was down to me, because he's still there and I'm out. The mind's a funny thing.'

She watched him for a time in silence. Then she said, 'I don't know anything about either of you, but I'll bet you're the one they could least do without.'

He felt as if the breath had been kicked out of his lungs. The private chats he'd had with DI Jones. 'Whiteley's aiming to fast-track you, Frank. I know you're working on your exams. You can do it. One day you'll be giving me orders, just watch . . . '

Terry Jones had been like a father to him, pushing him, encouraging him, bawling him out, always ready with his time and nip of Scotch. Crane knew he was good. Just as he knew Benson was average. A reliable plodder, a good mate, but no burning ambition and no mind for finessing the angles.

★   ★   ★

After they'd eaten, they went through to the living-room with the last glasses of wine.

'We've got to talk about you now, Colette.'

'I know. Well, I've thought it over and I think I'll go south. That would be the last thing they'd expect, yes? London. I'll be able to lose myself there. What do you think?'

'I think you'd be wrong in the head.'

She watched him in silence, as they sat each side of the fireplace, with its flowered screen. 'There's no easy way to say this,' he said, 'but I'm not going to go along with you running away. You've made your point with the police. You need more freedom, need to lead a fuller life. Well, spell that out to them and go back in the programme.'

She flushed. 'I thought you were on my

172

side. I'm not going back to living like that. No way. If you hadn't helped me I'd have gone anyway, you know that. I'm certain I can lose myself a bloody sight better than that lot can.'

'Look, the police really know what they're up against now. So they put more people on your case till they've nailed him. They'll not give in, not with two DCs beaten senseless.'

'*More* fucking coppers guarding me! You can't do this, we're not keen on you doing that. Another job in another crappy town. Letters only reaching me when every bugger in the station's had his greasy paws on them. Forget it.'

'The police think you've got two choices — '

'I keep telling you, I don't *care*. Being dead and being the un-dead, what's the difference? This way I've got a chance to live like a human being again.'

'Can't you see, if you disappear and contact *anyone*, Brewer or one of his people might threaten them with violence, to get an address out of them. You know Dora's already watching her back.'

'All right, all *right*. Christ, I'll not contact anyone. I'll cut myself off completely. It'll still be a hundred times better than the crappy life they've made me live.'

'The police aren't the enemy, for Christ's sake! You owe them. Two of their men kicked

173

shitless simply trying to protect you, keep you alive. I know it seems like being banged up, but just stick with it. Six months could make all the difference.'

'No, Frank,' she said, in a calmer voice. 'Don't go on, because I'm not going back. This evening, getting a few down, having a laugh with a bloke, you can't begin to know what it feels like. Well, I want my life back and I don't care what it takes.'

'I stuck my neck out bringing you here,' he said doggedly. 'Believe me, if there's one thing makes the police see red it's private men like me getting involved in their business. You know how angry they are about being given the slip.'

On the final leg of their flight to Gargrave, they'd stopped at a public phone-box and she'd rung the police. Mobiles were too easy to trace. They'd gone berserk. Had insisted she tell them where she was and that she stayed there till they'd picked her up; had she any idea of the trouble and expense she was causing them? She'd been polite but firm, had told them she'd spare them any more trouble and expense by living her own life from now on.

'Don't worry,' she said coldly, 'I'll keep your name out of it.'

'They already know I'm in it. The first

thing they'd do would be to try and contact me. They'll know you couldn't have made it alone.'

'I'd have had a bloody good try. And if I'd known you were going to rabbit on about this programme bollocks I would have done. Christ, they can take you out of the police force but they can't take the fucking police force out of you, can they.' She realized what she was saying, began to flush again. 'Sorree . . . sorree . . . that wasn't on . . . Oh, *shit!*'

He leant over, took her hand. 'All right, I helped you get away, brought you here. And you've hit the nail: I've got police force tattooed on my arse. But you've got to be protected. You could already be dead. He let you go once because he's a sadistic nutter who gets off on it. We can't give him another chance.'

'How can they get him till he tries to *attack* me?' she suddenly cried, her amber eyes glinting. 'You ask me, I think that's why the police let me go back to the office in the first place. So he'd have another go at me and they could pile in.'

There was no answer to that. It threw him. She'd worked it out for herself exactly the way he'd worked it out. She was a sharp kid.

'You know I'm right, don't you?' Her voice was still high-register. 'The only way they'll

175

ever nail him is if they can catch him at it. But I'd be dead anyway. I'll be dead whatever happens, so I might just as well do some living first, right?'

Crane stared bleakly into space. The trouble was, the logic seemed indestructible, the way Brewer worked. All the same. 'Colette, I'm begging you to give the programme one more go. I'll stay in touch. I might even be able to visit once the dust's settled.'

'Frank,' she said, in the steely tone he was getting used to, 'I'm . . . not . . . going . . . back.'

'Colette — '

'For Christ's *sake!*' she screamed. 'Can't you get it into your fucking head, no, no, *NO!*'

★ ★ ★

Crane lay in bed in the second bedroom. There were two on the first floor, a third built into the roof space, with a dormer. He'd left her without another word. There was nowhere else to go. So what now? He knew he'd be in serious trouble with the police if he didn't tell them everything he knew. And if he did, and they tracked her down, she'd spend the rest of her life hating his guts. He could never have believed the old Colette could have had such a pigheaded, strong-willed sister, who could make such unflinching decisions about life and death.

He heard the creak of a floorboard. He tensed, slid his legs out of the bed. He knew the house was secure, but . . . His bedroom door opened slowly with a slight whine of un-oiled hinges. He clenched his fists. He could just make out a shape in white. 'Are you asleep?' she whispered.

'You must be joking. Maybe I'd sleep when my pulse drops to a hundred.'

'I'm sorry. I didn't mean to give you a shock.'

She moved across to the bed. She'd carried a small case with her when she'd got into his car on Vicar Lane. The nightdress must have been in that.

'I didn't mean to shout at you. You're just about all I've got. None of this could have happened without you, I know that. I can be a stroppy bitch.'

He sighed. 'I can't make you do anything you don't want to do. I still felt I had to try. You've had a bad time and I care what happens to you.'

He heard a rustling sound and could just make out she was lifting the nightdress over her head.

'Will you give me a cuddle? You can't begin

to know how much I need one.'

She slid her soft sensuous body into his bed, with its musky scent, and Crane gave her a thorough cuddle. And then stood in for that clever, ambitious man she'd never get over, while she stood in for Vicky, the one whose leaving him, combined with losing his police career, had made him the man he'd become. Sad.

⋆ ⋆ ⋆

He was out of bed before she awoke. He shaved, showered, dressed, made coffee. She came down half an hour later. She was wearing stone-coloured trousers and a light-brown shirt.

'Hi,' she said, giving him a faint smile.

He was relieved. He'd been wary. But there'd been no black-out, no regression to an old, secure happiness. She was still in the here and now, poor kid. And he could tell she'd not changed her mind about anything. There was still a determined line to her mouth, a square, almost aggressive set to her shoulders. But she was very pale. It wasn't just because she wasn't made up. She lived with fear again. She'd been near-hyper last night with the excitement of it all, but this was another day.

She glanced through the living-room window. The weather was more settled after yesterday's broken pattern. The green glittered with dew and the cottages opposite had the look of timeless peace that summer heat and light seemed to bring out in ancient brickwork.

'Pity we're not a real couple and could go for that walk to the viaduct he was chuntering about.'

He nodded, put an arm round her. Such clear, settled weather for a homicidal maniac to be hunting an innocent young kid who endlessly mourned a fine young man.

'We'd better eat and go,' he said.

'I thought all you had was black coffee.'

'I do, but you don't.'

She gave him a sheepish grin. She was hungry, as usual. She'd probably want cereals and eggs and toast, and anyway he wanted her to have a decent breakfast against whatever the day might throw at her.

'Problem,' he said, 'there's nothing in the dairy line.'

'We could ask old Tom to sell us some milk and eggs.'

'I'll nip round.'

'No, let me. It's me who seems to need more than black coffee. Shan't be long.'

Crane couldn't explain it, but he didn't

want her to leave the house alone, even to go next door. He followed her, caught her arm. 'Hold on, Colette . . . ' They both reached the little hall together, and saw it together on the door-mat. It was a small plastic doll of the Cindy type, with metallic blonde hair and spikey little breasts and a bright blue dress. A long thin nail had been forced through the left breast and out the doll's back.

'Christ,' she whispered. 'Who could possibly . . . how could he *possibly*? No one followed us. How could he know I'd even *gone*?'

Her face was moist with shock. Bands of white flared round her pupils. A bead of sweat trickled down Crane's spine. She was right, how *could* he have pinned this house down when no car had shadowed his? Colette herself hadn't even known where they were going till they were halfway there.

'The old man,' he muttered.

She gave him a dazed glance.

'He was the only contact we made in this place.'

'You can't think it was *him*!' she cried, lips quivering.

'I don't know what to think.'

'What do we do? What do we *do*?'

'I'm going to see him. I need to check him out.'

180

'Don't leave me *here*!'

'See what I mean,' he shouted, 'about the programme? What chance have you got if he always knows where you are?'

She stared at him open-mouthed, as if he'd slapped her face. Fear seemed to blend with rage in her features, and she suddenly hurled the doll into the fireplace. 'Bastard!' she screamed. 'Bastard, bastard, *bastard*!'

Crane grabbed her hand and marched her to the house on the left. It seemed hard to believe the green and its line of houses could look so normal. Milk and papers were being delivered, a man cleaned his car, scraps of conversation could clearly be heard in the still air.

The cottage doors opened directly on to the pavement. He rang the bell. There was no response. He rang it again. It was in working order but he still didn't answer. He knocked on the door then, loudly. It could be he was hard of hearing.

A door opened to the left of the old man's. A small, plump woman with greying ginger hair and glasses, and wearing an apron, looked out at them. 'I'm sure he's in,' she said, with a puzzled frown. 'He's always in in the morning. He's getting on, you know. Was it anything in particular, only if you're Jehovahs I shouldn't bother. He's RC. Very devoted. Used to take the plate round till he started with his hip.'

'We're staying at Mr Green's cottage,' Crane told her. 'Mr Bower came round last night, wanting to know if we needed anything. Milk, eggs. I said I'd let him know this morning.'

She looked even more confused. 'That's very strange. I'm the one who sees to Mr and Mrs Green. I've got keys, don't you see, give the place a tidy-up and so forth.'

He watched her uneasily. It was what he'd been afraid of, even though he couldn't give the fear any shape. 'Would you have a key to Mr Bower's?'

'Had one ever since their Annie died, God rest her. They said someone should have a key, keep an eye on him.'

'I really think it might be best if we check on him, Mrs . . . ?'

'Benson, dear. Ivy. Like the bandleader. Very big in the forties, but it won't mean a thing to you young folk. I do hope he's all right. He's been known to sleep in if he's been watching the cricket. I don't think that pipe does him a scrap of good.'

She scuttled inside, came back with a key attached by garden twine to an empty cotton-bobbin. She opened the door and they all went in. The place smelt of cat, old carpets and dry rot. He must have lit a coal fire last evening, in the grate of the old fireplace, which had a dark-oak surround and picture tiles. It had burnt itself out to cinder and ash.

He sat in front of it in an armchair of cracked and faded leather, apparently asleep. But they all knew he was dead. Ivy Benson gave a little scream and put a hand to her cheek.

Crane guessed he'd been dead some time. And despite his intense unease, the death looked to be completely natural. It looked to be the type of death that followed a stroke, as his mouth was drawn down to one side.

But it wasn't the Tom Bower who'd called on them last night. Similar, very similar, but not the same.

10

Lenny watched the activity across the green from his souped-up Focus, parked among a scattering of other cars. He'd attached a short beard to his face today and wore a fair-haired wig. He also wore a checked shirt, moleskin pants and a cloth cap. The horsy look he'd told himself earlier, with his thin smile. He waited patiently, looking forward to when they went inside. He'd not be surprised if the sight of old Tom gave the old lass a heart attack too.

Not that he'd wanted old Tom to do a flat-line. He could do without dead bodies, too much trouble and mess. He only ever whacked people when he had to. But it had all been too much for old Tom in the end. He'd not been able to handle the shock when Lenny had taken out the length of washing-line. Poor guy. Reminded Lenny of his grandad. But he *was* bloody old. Not long to go anyway, by the sound of that cough. Blessing in disguise really.

Lenny didn't think the gumshoe would hang around once it was all over. Where to next? Lenny had other ideas for keeping up the pressure on Colette Jennings. The gumshoe must be crapping himself by now wondering how he did it. Always knowing where they were. Lenny gave a little chuckle. There was a café in the village where he'd be able to get something to eat. There was plenty of time. They'd need to get a doctor in and tell the pigs. 'See you later, folks,' he muttered.

★　★　★

They were on the move again, driving along dappled roads past the patchwork of fields, where animals grazed and crops glowed yellow and white-painted farmsteads stood sharply etched in the clear light. The road was busy, Saturday morning busy, with relaxed drivers cruising to supermarkets and garden parties and antique sales, as they sang along to feel-good music. *He'd* almost certainly be in one of those cars, even if he was nowhere in sight. He'd never been anywhere in sight yesterday but he'd still known how to reach a cottage in a village in a corner of North Yorkshire.

'Are you . . . checking cars out?' she said, in a low voice.

'Not any more.'

He glanced from the wheel, saw her give a

resigned nod. What was the point?

'Where are we going?'

'Nowhere. Anywhere. I just need time to think.'

'What happened, Frank? What could have *happened*? Who was the old man who came to see *us*?'

'Brewer. Got to be. We already knew he could do voices. Well, now we know he can handle a make-up box. A grey wig, a touching of grease-paint for the wrinkles, the metal-framed glasses, the stoop. And he's not all that tall, according to Adam at Jarvis Motors. And he was standing in darkness. So he had us fooled.'

'But how could he possibly have known about the old man? And what did he do to him? It *seemed* natural, him dying like that, but — '

'Brewer spots my car outside Jeremy's place, yes? He looks round. It was getting dark and he's trained to move like a shadow. Maybe he sees Tom pottering about in his front room. The old man has the lights on but hasn't drawn the curtains yet. So then let's say Brewer rings his bell and smooth talks his way into the house. He does good smooth talk and it's a quiet village where people still trust one another. Let's say he gets him going about Jeremy's cottage. He must have worked out we're using it to hole up in and so it's probably someone's second home. Maybe he asks Tom who owns it so he can maybe rent it. Tom's probably lonely since his wife died and he's glad of this nice bloke to have a natter with.'

Crane stopped at a junction and waited for a gap in the right-moving traffic. They were on the outskirts of Skipton, which was always busy on Saturdays, when the wide high street was lined for the day with tented stalls.

'Then . . . what?' She sounded as if she didn't really want to know.

'I think Brewer tells him he wants to borrow some of his clothes and use his bathroom. Maybe he says he'll need to tie him to his chair till he's done what he has to do. He'd not want him dead, that's for sure. Brewer isn't that kind of killer. He simply wanted a borrow of his clothes.

'I reckon Tom died of shock. It wouldn't be what Brewer wanted, but on the other hand dead men don't talk. So he just carried on with the game. We actually saw him this time. The doll was to make sure you knew.'

Trembling, she clasped and unclasped her hands. He drove on to a roundabout at the top of the high street, then took a left on a climbing road that led to Bolton Abbey. It took Crane back. He'd hiked up there as a youth, walking through Westy Bank Woods to the high moorland. But he dragged his mind back to focus on what needed to be done now, after he'd put a certain theory to the test.

Ivy Benson had called the police, who'd begun the sudden-death procedure that Crane knew well. The old man's doctor had been alerted and a single uniformed policeman had arrived in a panda. They'd taken over and Crane, Colette and Ivy had gone back to Jeremy's place. Ivy had made very strong tea on auto-pilot and poured them cups. She kept saying she was sure the pipe hadn't helped, never had it out of his mouth, and that she'd known him since she was knee-high to a daisy, and their Annie.

Crane, struggling to get it together, had made sympathetic noises. Colette had stared into space with the haunted look he remembered so well from Blackbird Common. The PC had come round then, while the doctor made arrangements for disposal of the body. He was young, fresh-faced, and took a relaxed view of the death. He'd have been there to look on while the doctor made his examination, to ensure the body was unmarked, with no signs of interference or foul play. There obviously hadn't been, which made Crane certain Tom had died of shock.

Ivy had begun to cry. The policeman put a hand on her arm and said gently, 'These things happen, love. It would have been very quick. Little or no pain. And being a widower, blessing in disguise, wouldn't you say?'

He'd taken brief statements from them. Crane had touched Colette's ankle with his shoe and explained how the old man had come round the night before with his offer of milk and eggs. As far as the police were concerned, he was sticking to the line that Tom and Brewer were one and the same. The truth could only make things even more impossibly complicated than they already were. The old man had simply died, as old men did.

There had been tense seconds when Ivy had said tremulously, through her tears, 'I can't *understand* it . . . Tom coming round to see this lady and gentleman about milk and eggs. I see to all that, he *knew* that. Took him all his time to look after himself, and the cat.'

'He'd be confused, love,' the young officer said, in a kindly tone. 'It often happens when they're getting on. They get funny ideas, want to feel they're still useful. We had the same problem with my old grandad . . . '

Crane swung off the Bolton Abbey road on to the A65, a route that led across more fine country, past the Chelker reservoir, still as glass, through small villages drowsing in the sun, until he drove into Ilkley at the foot of the moor. There was a car-park behind the high street, where he paid and displayed.

'Where now?'

'Betty's,' he said. 'You'd better have something to eat, seeing as we never did get those milk and eggs.'

She looked relieved. Brewer pretending to be old Tom, a stabbed doll, a dead man, she badly needed her comfort food. He led her through an alley from the car-park on to a road called The Grove. It was a place of fashion, antique and bookshops, estate agents and a garden where the elderly sat on benches. Betty's combined a patisserie with a restaurant, and smelt of ground coffee and freshly baked bread. They were shown to a window table in a long crowded room that gave a view over rooftops to the rising land towards Middleton, its copses and villas and folds of land sharp-edged in the clear air.

She ordered a Swiss rosti based on bacon, with a mixed salad and French fries. Crane's normal lunch was a sandwich, but he didn't want her to feel more self-conscious about her food craving than she already was. He ordered the haddock. When the dishes arrived and they'd begun to eat, he said, 'Well, *do* you go back in the programme? You've seen what he's capable of.'

'How could he have traced us? It doesn't seem possible . . . '

Crane glanced towards the crowded car-park, diagonally below them to the right, the brightwork of cars glittering in the sun. He had an idea he might know how Brewer did it very soon, but he couldn't be certain and didn't want to talk about it at this stage.

'I don't know. I've given it a lot of thought.'

'I've done a lot of thinking myself. I'm still not going back to the programme.' She spooned more of the dressed salad on to her plate, gave him an edgy glance. 'I rang Dora this morning. On my mobile in the bathroom, just before we set off. Told her what I've decided to do. She wants me to go and live with her. They've killed her son and Harry's gone and she has to be on the look-out when she drives anywhere. That's why her nerves gave out. But she's back at home now and says she could face life better if I was with her. That goes for me too.'

He watched her in a lengthy silence. Then he said bluntly, 'You need to be sectioned. You're going to live in *Woking*. Where Donny has his business. Where Lenny has his pad. For Christ's sake, you'd be saying come and get me!'

'I don't care,' she said, in a low voice. 'I keep telling you but the penny never drops. I don't care and neither does she. They've ruined both our lives. We were always close. We have a lot to give each other. We can share the pain and we can share the fear. We'll be support for each other. The way we see it we've nothing to lose.'

'Think the police will let you live openly down there?' he said. 'It makes no sense and you know it.'

'I'm not the fucking criminal!' she burst out, her fork clattering on her plate. 'It wasn't me going crackers with a knife!'

Her voice pierced the buzz of general conversation, and an elderly couple glanced at her in alarm from a nearby table.

'Not so *loud* — '

'Well, I'm *not*,' she hissed, flushing. 'I don't have to stay in the fucking programme and they can't make me.'

'You'd be signing your own death warrant.'

'No one understands,' she said, in a voice he could hardly hear now. 'Not even you. I've lost my bloke and my friends and my family, and she's lost her son and her husband. All we've really got now is each other.'

'Look.' He put a hand on her arm. 'You've *got* to see it from their side. The police. They've *got* to keep you safe. How would it look to the public if Brewer got to you and they seemed to be sitting on their hands?'

'They'll just have to follow me around, Frank. Like they follow the Royals. Because what life I've got left is going to be my own.'

★   ★   ★

'All right,' he said, as they walked along The Grove's wide pavement, 'I've said my last word. We did all the arguing last night. It was just that with Brewer knocking on the door . . . the doll . . . Tom dead . . . well, I just had to give it one more shot. I know you don't care. I know nothing will make you go back in the programme. Well, if it's any consolation, I think maybe I'd feel the same.'

She grasped his hand. It seemed to Crane they must have looked like any other couple strolling on The Grove, whose only worry was could they afford the mortgage. She said, 'If you didn't care you'd not get so angry with me, I realize that, Frank.'

'Promise me one thing: you'll let the Woking police know the minute you're through Dora's door.'

She nodded, with a bitter smile. 'I do *want* to go on living, you know, whatever you must think of the stroppy bitch you've saddled yourself with.'

Crane knew her chances to go on living were not good whatever she did. She knew it too, with a fatalism that was near-indestructible. Some would think her courageous, some would think her a bloody fool. In the end she was maybe just being herself, the confident blonde who'd always lived her own way, to the full.

They walked down the alley, back to the big car-park, then threaded their way through the dense lines of vehicles. Crane had had two reasons for stopping off in Ilkley. One, to make sure she had a decent meal, two, to leave the car unattended for at least an hour. It was an open invitation to Brewer to leave more evidence that he still knew where they were. If he did, Crane would know how he did it. They came in sight of the Megane. Crane had an idea there'd be a note under a windscreen wiper, or stuck to the windscreen like a traffic warden's ticket. If that had been the case, he aimed to distract her attention so he could palm it into his pocket. She'd had too many shocks in the last forty-eight hours.

There was nothing attached to the windscreen. But when they got closer he felt his spirits drop. And it was too late now to distract her. She was already making her way round the car to the passenger door. Her mouth dropped open in shock. There was an elaborate mourning wreath on the passenger seat.

A card, edged in black, was laid on top. It had been printed in black ink with the message: IN LOVING MEMORY OF COLETTE JENNINGS AKA JANE KENNEDY.

Brewer still knew where they were.

11

He drove rapidly on a winding road that passes along the side of the River Wharfe and would take them to Leeds. The wreath had given her another massive shock. The pallor was back and the shaking hands, but he knew her determination was still intact. Maybe even stronger.

She finally spoke, through trembling lips. 'How could he get in your car?'

'Breaking into a Megane would be a piece of piss to someone with his skills.'

'How can he *always* know where we are?'

'Somewhere in my car he's planted a transmitter. He'd got my office address from Adam and it wouldn't have taken long for him to pin down my car. The car gets parked all over the place when I'm working in the city, including multistoreys. He fits a transmitter in mine and his car will have a receiver. So then he doesn't actually need to see my car, he just goes by the strength of the signal he picks up. With his money, skills and contacts he might even have got his hands on the sort of equipment that can place a car's position within yards by satellite.'

'If . . . if you thought he'd planted something in your car why didn't you look for it this morning, before we left Gargrave? Or in Ilkley? It must be still *going*!'

He took his eyes from the road for a second to glance at her. 'Because I'd not have known what I was looking for. You know how much gear they cram under the bonnet these days. I'd not know one gadget from another, and it'll look as grimy as all the rest now with all the driving I do and all the road dust thrown up through the chassis frame.'

'I . . . we can't get away from him then,' she said, 'whatever we do.'

'I've got an idea that might work,' he said. 'I have to see how things are when we get there.'

They didn't speak again until they were driving into Leeds. As he'd hoped, it was dense with shopping-day traffic. He began to circle the streets of the centre. She said, 'Shouldn't you have turned right back there for the station?'

He glanced at the car clock. 'I know where it is, Colette. There's a London train at three-five. I'm aiming to get to the station about five to. I'll drop you at the concourse, then drive on. We know Brewer's behind us somewhere and we also know he's not going to get too close. With luck he'll not see you being dropped. I drive out of Leeds then and on to Leeds-Bradford airport. The plan is, he'll think circling round Leeds was a deliberate plan to confuse him, and that you're really flying somewhere. By the time he finds you're not you'll be halfway to London.'

'I keep forgetting how carefully you work things out.'

'Call it experience.'

'I reckon you must have been a bloody good cop.'

He shrugged. 'Water under the bridge.'

She said, 'He might have a go at you to find out where I've really gone.'

'I doubt it. He'll have guessed I have connections and he doesn't want any more trouble than he can help. I'm guessing he'll be certain I'll keep in touch with you. I don't think he'll have twigged I've figured out how he managed to follow me around. In any case it won't matter soon when his people tell him you're back in Surrey.'

He made his final circuit and now drove along the street that led to the railway station from the rear on a one-way system. 'Right,' he said briskly, 'grab your case and the second I pull in leg it on to the concourse. You'll just have time to buy a ticket. The London train nearly always leaves from platform five, bang up to the barrier. Goodbye . . . and all the luck in the world.'

He pulled in. She paused only to throw her arms round him and kiss him. 'I'll never forget you and all you've done for me . . . '

Then she was gone, darting through the crowd, a beige lightweight jacket now part of the earlier combination of shirt and trousers. She looked like any other young woman rushing off to London, maybe to catch a show or party with friends. Crane sighed. Poor kid. Knowing the fear would never end. Knowing her new-found freedom would only last till a murdering sadist made his final move. Even if the police did follow her around. Like the Royals.

★　★　★

Leeds-Bradford was situated in open country just beyond a village called Yeadon. Some of the locals still called it Yeadon airport. It was roughly at the centre of a triangle the points of which were Leeds, Bradford and Harrogate. When Lenny drove on to the A658 and saw a big silvery aircraft just floating upwards into a clear sky above the pattern of fields he smiled his thin smile. The bitch was aiming to *fly* somewhere! Crane had just been playing silly buggers in Leeds, driving in circles. Well, he knew his game now. He'd hoped Lenny would be thrown off track when the real destination was this airport. Lenny took a right at a roundabout and drove along the lane that led to the airport itself. As he drove into the car-park he spotted Crane's car almost immediately. Still dressed in his country gear, wigged and bearded, he walked rapidly to the airport complex, then slowed to a stroll to move cautiously into the lounge. A casual glance showed him that Crane was sitting there, reading a paper. But where was the bitch? In the toilets, where else? Women were *always* in the toilets.

Lenny sat down at some distance from Crane in the busy lounge, but where he could keep an eye on him. Crane read steadily for a good ten minutes, but still no sign of the bloody woman. She had to be somewhere around. He carefully checked out every other woman in the lounge, and he knew her both as a blonde and a brunette, but there was no one there who looked remotely like her. Was she in some departure lounge? Why wasn't Crane seeing her off? What was going on? Why was he just sitting there? He'd never been apart from the stupid slut since last evening. Lenny was becoming very distracted, but his training helped him keep it under wraps. Had she already taken a flight? No, they needed to check in early these days and they'd not been here long enough. What the *fuck* was going on? He'd aimed to pin down the flight she was taking and perhaps buying a spot ticket for the same plane. At least he'd know which part of the country she was flying *to*. And he knew she was a financial adviser and it wouldn't take long to check out the limited number of firms who'd employ her.

But Lenny was beginning to smell a rat. He could have taken a degree in smelling a rat. At the end of another ten minutes he knew Crane had pulled a fast one. Shit! All that circling round in Leeds. Maybe he *had* dropped her off somewhere. Somewhere like Leeds fucking railway station!

Shit, shit, shit, *shit*! Lenny got casually to his feet as if to go to the toilets himself, but once out of sight of Crane he made off from the building and back to the car-park. Not that Crane would be able to place a bearded man with a cloth cap as Lenny Brewer among the crowd in the lounge, but that was the painstaking way Lenny operated. Once in the car, he allowed himself to clench his hands in trembling fury. It could take him weeks now, months even, to get another lead on the twat who'd put the old man inside.

'You'll pay for this,' he spat. 'Both of you!'

Benson had the guarded look he always seemed to have around Crane these days, as he stood at the half-open front door.

'We need to talk, Ted.'

Benson glanced back into the house uneasily.

'Out here, if you like.'

'I've got the in-laws here. It's awkward . . . '

But he came out reluctantly and led the way to the back garden, which was mainly lawn with a children's play area at the bottom and hedged off with beech bushes. Crane told him everything that had happened during the last twenty-four hours, apart from the death of Tom Bower.

Benson, smoking as usual, listened as they stood in declining sunlight, shooting Crane startled glances, his mouth set in a taut line.

'You're *crackers*!' he said, when Crane had finished. '*Helping* her! Helping her get away from the police! The programme! They'll go ballistic! Christ, they had a chance of nailing him if they'd known he was following you. You must know the shed-load of no good you've done yourself. She *can't* just walk away from the programme.'

'She stopped seeing the point of the

programme when Brewer made dogmeat of the guards,' Crane said evenly.

'He'd never have got near her if she'd not sent you fart-arsing to Woking.'

'She knows that now. But she's convinced Brewer will get to her anyway, however well she's guarded.'

'Stupid slag — '

'The point is,' Crane cut him off, 'I'm of exactly the same mind, that she shouldn't have left the programme. All the time I've been with her has been spent trying to persuade her to think again. She was going to leg it whether I helped her or not. So I helped her, because I didn't want her to end up a dead body in a back street. I took her to Gargrave deliberately, so I had the time and the place to talk some sense into her.'

Benson flicked his cigarette into a border, lit a new one. 'What a fucking mess. I wish to Christ I'd never given her your name in the first place. You should have told them everything she was aiming to do, every foot of the way.'

'It's happened now. What's the point of twenty-twenty hindsight?'

'It means that what help you've had from the police in the past will now be just about non-existent.'

'Not if you put my side.'

'What's that supposed to mean?'

'That I want you to tell Terry Jones what I've told you. That I acted for the best, did everything I could to get her to see reason about the programme. I need someone with Terry's clout to speak to the Leeds police and put my side.'

'Why not speak to them yourself? The horse's mouth.'

'Because they'd tear me apart. You know that. A private man fucking about in their business. But Terry would know how to handle it.'

'I don't want to get involved, Frank. Life is complicated enough as it is. Why not go to Terry direct?'

'Because you're my contact, Ted, and I didn't want you to think I was keeping you out of the loop.'

Crane turned away abruptly and took several steps across the lawn. He had rarely been so angry and didn't want Ted to see his anger. He turned, watched Benson in silence for a time.

'How's your wife's health these days?' he said. 'Better than it was, I hope.'

Benson reddened, looked away. 'She copes,' he muttered. 'They do their best but there's no real cure so far.'

They both stood in another silence, still

apart, as the low sun reflected itself in blinding points of light in distant windows across the valley. There was the sound of a patio door being drawn. '*Frank!*' a voice called. 'Lovely to *see* you! Why didn't you tell me it was Frank, Ted? It's been such a long time.' She came out on to the lawn, a small dark-haired woman with the rather fragile looks some chronic asthmatics developed. She put her arms round him and kissed him on the cheek. 'Oh, it's *good* to see you. You must come for a drink or a meal sometime, like the old days. We do miss you, don't we, Ted, not to mention the kids.'

'Blame it on the workload, Teresa. But I will come soon. How are you keeping?'

'I'm holding my own. They're trying me on some new medication.'

'I'll speak to Terry, Frank,' Benson suddenly cut in. 'I'll give him a ring now . . .'

★   ★   ★

Terry Jones also had company to dinner, but he broke off and led Benson into a little room he used as a study. He listened with his usual impassive face as the other told him Crane's story. 'I said what a bloody fool he'd been, said he should have kept us informed every foot of the way. He says he tried to talk her into going back, that he only helped her clear off because she'd have cleared off anyway. But, well, it's pretty obvious he's involved with her and maybe not using his head. I told him straight he'd done himself no good with us. That's what's bugging him. Wants you to put his side to the Leeds people.'

Jones nodded, thought. 'All right, Ted, leave it with me. I'll get on to them right away. At least they'll know where she's heading.' He glanced at his watch. 'Should be at the Dora woman's place by now. And you're right, Crane shouldn't have gone it alone. He of all people should know what's police business and what isn't. But if he was acting for the best maybe we should take a lenient view . . .'

★ ★ ★

Jones watched Benson walk down the drive and get in his car. He closed the door and stood in the hall. A murmur of voices came from the dining-room. He'd had to break off from his meal, but what was new for a DI? His guests were used to it. He wondered what it was between Benson and Crane. They'd once been close friends as well as colleagues who always tried to work together. The closeness seemed to have ended when Crane was dismissed, though he knew they kept in touch. Jones didn't care for the holier-than-thou attitude Benson had gradually begun to take about Crane. Crane had messed up on a grand scale, but he'd taken it on the chin the way he took everything else, and he'd been one of the best coppers Jones had ever known.

So what was Benson's problem? Why had he begun to take this narrow official line with a man he'd once taken home to dinner? It wasn't a train of thought he was too keen to pursue. The vague outline of dubious motives in Benson's behaviour might begin to take clearer shape. He sighed. Two good men, a sharp one who could think on his feet, and a reliable plodder you could trust to tie up the loose ends. They'd made a great team.

He was certain of one thing, and Benson had to be left in no doubt about it. They went on helping Crane all they could. Jones knew Crane. Knew that if Crane said he'd helped Colette Jennings to clear off because she'd have cleared off anyway that would be the exact truth. And maybe he *had* been giving the kid one, but that wouldn't have clouded his judgement. Because nothing ever had.

And Crane would now be a worried man, Benson had been right about that at least. He needed his police contacts, because there were a dozen ways they could help him, nudge nudge, putting work his way, keeping him in touch with the right people, slipping him info it would take hours to dig out for himself. It had given Crane a big boost in getting his agency off the blocks. And Crane must now be thinking he'd blown it so badly over the Jennings affair that he'd be in danger of being frozen out. Which was what his one-time mate Benson seemed to have threatened him with.

And which was something Jones was going to ensure didn't happen. Christ, he wished Crane was back.

★　★　★

Not long after Crane got home, the phone rang.

'I'm here. At Dora's.'

'No problems?'

'None.'

'And you've told the local police?'

'I've only just got here — '

'You promised to ring them the minute you were through the door.'

'They'll be round here like blue-arsed flies.'

'You've got to tell them, Colette. The minute we ring off. They've got to be put in the picture and they have to know you're

208

taking responsibility for your own actions.'

'Oh, all right.'

'Don't let me down. I have to know they're keeping an eye on you.'

'I won't, Frank,' she said, a gentler note in her husky voice.

'Maybe I'll come and see you one day. When you're settled in.'

'I'd like that.'

'How's Dora?'

'*So* pleased I'm here. You can't believe. It was just great seeing her again after all this time. We haven't stopped talking since I got here. We're . . . it's like a new lease of life.'

He thought about it later. He could understand the kid being in a state of euphoria, having made it clear to Woking, but Dora? She'd needed to go in a clinic because her nerves were in such a state. He'd have thought the last thing she could cope with was to have Colette under the same roof, a woman they both knew was a certain target for a ruthless killer.

He couldn't get it together.

★   ★   ★

Crane worked from home at the weekend. They were good days for catching people unawares, people who owed other people large sums of money, people who were living very lavishly on salaries their employers knew didn't match the lifestyle, landlords who were indenting for benefit claimants who seemed to outnumber the available rooms.

He'd just finished the black coffee that was all he had at breakfast-time, and was getting ready to go, when the doorbell rang. It was Terry Jones.

'Hello, Frank, long time no see.'

Crane smiled wryly. 'I hope it's not another bollocking, Terry. I had it from Ted Benson.'

'Can I come in?'

Crane took him through to the front living-room. It was little changed from the days when his parents had owned the house. He'd bought it from them when they'd gone to live on the coast. It still had the old leather suite and the display cabinet, the fifteen-year-old telly and the chocolate-boxy pictures on the wall. It suited Crane.

'No bollocking, Frank. I know you did what you did for the right reasons.'

Crane nodded. 'I've just made this coffee if you'd like a cup.'

'No. This'll not take long. The thing is, Frank, I know you; the Leeds people don't and they're very angry. That's putting it mildly. They think you should have kept them in the picture every foot of the way. If you had done they think they had the best chance they're going to get of nailing Brewer.'

'They don't know what they're up against. He's fought in African wars. He can impersonate people, put on voices, knows how to bug cars. That's how he could follow me so easily.'

'I told them all that. I also told them that when you were in the force you were the best DS I ever had. I told them you did everything you could to get her to go back under cover. You only helped her do a runner because she'd have done a runner anyway.'

'Thanks, Terry. I knew you could sort it. They'd have made dogmeat of me if I'd gone direct.'

'All right, I've calmed them down.' He smiled faintly. 'I think what really bugged them was the way she walked past them looking like Marilyn Monroe and got away with it.'

He looked over Crane's garden, also unchanged since his parents' day, and which Crane paid a pensioner to 'tidy up'. 'Anyway, they're liaising with the Woking police about her staying with this Dora. They think she's being a selfish fucking bitch. I quote.'

'What'll happen in Woking?'

'We're in a grey area. They can't get it together about her wanting to abandon the programme, the obvious danger she's in, but they can't *force* her back into it. They'll not stop trying, that goes without saying.'

'They'll be wasting their time.'

'They're seriously worried about their image. They know how very bad it'll look for them if Brewer does get to her. Field day for the media, who thought they'd just about squeezed everything out of the murder and the trial and her needing protection.'

'More worried about their image than the revenge-killing of the kid herself, I suppose.'

Crane caught a trace of the hard look Jones could get in his eyes when nothing else in his face moved. 'Come on, Frank, get in the real world. They are sorry for her, but if she'll not do exactly as she's told she becomes a dangerous nuisance.'

Crane sighed, nodded. 'I know. It's just that she's been to hell and back. Not just her bloke being killed in front of her but having to live as if she's in prison herself.'

'It's the only way, until they can get Brewer. Well, we both know that.' His steady gaze met Crane's again. 'Look, I've suggested something to the Leeds people that will do you a bit of good. Show them your heart's in the right place. Why don't you go down to Dora's next weekend and have one last crack at talking Colette into seeing sense?'

Crane grimaced. 'Christ, Terry, I spent the entire weekend doing little else.'

'I know that. But one last shot? It would look good. It would bear out all the positive things I said about you.'

Crane knew he'd have to go. Favours were being called in. He could guess at the hidden agenda. When the press picked up Colette living openly the police could say they'd done everything possible to make her stay under cover, even shipped in her boyfriend to talk sense into her. What more could they have done? They couldn't *force* her underground. She was free to make her own choices, even crazy ones.

Crane also knew the situation had advantages for the police. If Colette insisted on making herself an obvious target they'd have a better chance of pinning down Brewer. And this time they'd be having her shadowed by the best people they'd got, people as skilled in the arts of stealth and hair-trigger reactions as Brewer himself.

'All right, Terry,' he said, sighing again, 'I'll give it one last shot.'

'Good man. You'll find us very grateful,' he said, with a meaningful glance, 'back at the station.'

Relieved by these words, Crane saw Jones

to the door. The other hesitated, turned. 'I don't want to reopen old wounds, Frank, but if you *had* to fix evidence against that piece of human shite, I could never see anyone as sharp as you getting it wrong.'

Crane wouldn't have got it wrong. But he'd trusted Benson with a crucial part of the detailed work, and it had been a flaw in that detail the legal people had picked up on. 'Just one of those things, Terry,' he said flatly.

But their glances met, and Jones knew that Crane's was telling a different story. 'Well,' he said, 'best of luck, old son.' He took Crane's hand warmly in both his own. 'And thanks for agreeing to go.'

★   ★   ★

The following Friday afternoon Crane was on the road south again, his car now debugged. Stan at Jarvis Motors had a mental map of the engine compartment of every Renault, and had rapidly pinned down the tiny transmitter and removed it. Not that it mattered much now that Colette was back in Woking. As he drove, Crane wondered if her non-negotiable decision to live openly might not have a lot to do with Tony, the man she'd never get over. If the worst came to the worst and she did lose her life she'd be where he was. Crane hated it, hated to see her as he was almost certain she was beginning to see herself. A dead woman walking.

12

He drove into Woking and joined the stream of traffic surging along the main road skirting the canal, then swung left to take the route to the rear of the railway station, and beyond it Eastern Lane. It was as closely lined with cars as before and he parked the Megane in a nearby multi-storey.

He walked back towards Dora's semi. He was certain Brewer would now be back in Woking also. Maybe it was even a kind of disappointment to a twisted sod like Brewer that Colette had made herself such an easy target. It was clear he'd been getting off on the challenge of keeping her in his sights. Crane still hadn't worked out how Brewer had cottoned on to him in the first place. Maybe he never would. He shrugged, turned into the drive of Dora's place, rang the bell. There was no response for some time, but he was expecting that. He'd given Colette no warning that he was coming. He'd needed to take her unawares, needed to make some judgement of her state of mind after a week in the open. If she was beginning to feel jittery and even more vulnerable than usual there might be a slight chance he could talk her round. But he strongly doubted it.

There was a viewing glass in the door, and the delay would be due to Dora looking through it first, and then Colette. It was Colette who finally opened the door, looking very worried. The other woman stood behind her.

'Frank! What's happened? Come in . . . '

He joined them in the hallway. Dora Powell also looked very tense. 'This is Frank Crane, Dora, the man I've told you so much about. What *is* it, Frank?'

'Please come through . . . Frank,' Dora said, leading the way into the living-room. It was bright and spacious and tastefully furnished: a beige carpet and an oriental rug in front of a marble fireplace. Gold pencil-pleat curtains, a three-seater sofa and comfortable armchairs, a television in a reproduction cabinet, landscape paintings on the walls. It made a big contrast to the stark-looking rooms in the house on Blackbird Common. Crane guessed Colette must have come back here with a sigh of relief.

Dora said, 'Do sit down, Frank.'

'It's got to be something very serious to bring you all this way,' Colette said anxiously, turning towards him on the big sofa. Dora perched on the edge of one of the armchairs.

217

'Are you . . . both all right?'

'We're coping. We're not finding it easy, but we're coping. I could have told you that over the phone. What is it, Frank, really?'

He glanced from Colette to Dora, trying to gauge their true mental state. Dora wasn't what he'd expected. Colette had once described her as being about five-six with dark hair, blue-grey eyes and a *retroussé* nose. He'd thought she'd look middle-aged and matronly, a bit on the heavy side. She didn't. She had a slender, youthful frame, a pale, unlined face and long black hair. The hair could have been coloured, but it had been expertly done. It was difficult to believe the two women were a generation apart. Only the nerviness was left of the woman he'd imagined. She seemed to vibrate with it. There was also an impression of timidity, a lack of self-confidence. It wasn't surprising she'd been so close to a nervous breakdown. Crane still couldn't understand why she'd been so willing to have Colette live with her.

'I'm sorry,' he said finally. 'I didn't mean to give you a shock. There's no easy way of saying this. The police are convinced that after a week living openly you'll have become so jumpy you'll be ready to think again about going back in the programme. They've sent me to have one last go at talking you into it.'

She glanced at Dora, turned back to watch him in silence for a short time. 'I suppose the police were furious — about you helping me get away.'

'They laid off when I agreed to come down here. The local police have been round, I suppose.'

'They were here within minutes of Colette phoning them,' Dora broke in. 'They were very angry too, but I told them it was utterly absurd she should be made to live like someone in an open prison because she'd helped put away the man who'd murdered my son. I said they knew perfectly well it was Lenny Brewer doing those dreadful things to her, so why didn't they lock him up, not her.'

It threw Crane, the incredible protective vehemence that lay behind the timid manner. He said, 'They'd have to find him first, Dora.'

'Frank,' Colette said. There was affection in her amber eyes. 'I'm sorry they've made you come all this way. Nothing's changed. Dora and me, we're facing it out.'

'Are you quite happy with that, Dora?' he said evenly.

She still perched on the extreme edge of the armchair. She was like a bird on a lawn, alert for instant flight. 'She *couldn't* go on living like that, hardly daring to cross the doorstep, watched over day and night. It upset me so badly, hearing her on the phone. She'd changed out of all recognition. If you could only have known her before — ' She broke off and the two exchanged a fond glance that briefly excluded him.

Colette was wearing a lacy top in gold, made from a sort of metallic thread, with damson-coloured trousers. They'd be the type of clothes she'd loved to wear in the past. The roots of her blonde hair were beginning to show again in the centre parting. Maybe she was going to let the brown colouring grow out now and to hell with it.

'The thing is, Dora,' he said, 'there's absolutely no question Colette will be seriously at risk if she stays openly with you. You might both be. I know what close friends you are, but would you want her exposed to that kind of danger?'

'Our minds are made up, Frank,' she said bluntly. 'All we've got now is each other. We've talked it through a dozen times. We've suffered enough, just by Tony's death, and we don't see why we should take any more punishment. We'll never get over losing him, but we deserve the right to mourn him in peace together.'

Her hands shook slightly. She lived in great fear. But Crane had found that bravery and fear were sometimes two sides of the same coin. He had an idea she'd located a level of bravery in herself she'd not known was there.

'The Brewers don't care about any of that, Dora. Theirs is an upside-down world. The rackets and the killings, they're proud of themselves for getting rich on them. In their eyes, Tony's murder was his own fault, for upsetting Donny. To them, Colette's the guilty party, for putting Donny inside. They think it stands to reason she should have a contract on her head.'

Dora nodded slowly. Her gaze unfocused, she seemed to be thinking his words over carefully. Maybe, if he stuck with this hard line, there'd be a chance of getting her on his side. But then she said, 'If she went back in the programme we'd have lost. Don't you see? The Brewers would have taken her partner *and* her freedom. They'd have proved that they control things, not the police, not the rest of us who live decent lives. We've both had enough, Frank, of not just living in fear but living like outcasts.'

'The fear won't end, Dora. How can it?'

She glanced at Colette again. A fear shared seemed to be a fear halved. Crane wondered what the original attraction between them had been, the bubbly, self-assured, sexy blonde and the reserved and diffident older woman. They were like those pairs of girls he'd seen as a teenager, the outgoing flirty one and the plain shyer one, who tagged along with the other in the hope some of the glitter would rub off.

Could that have been the basis of their closeness, even across the age gap? For Dora, a friend who made her feel young again and was fun to be with, for Colette, a warm and admiring companion who would always be there for her. It was a powerful combination. He didn't think either had needed to talk the other into letting Colette come back here to live. They'd both wanted it.

'I do wish you'd rung first, Frank,' Colette said, with a rueful smile. 'I could have told you what you'd be up against.'

He shrugged. 'They have me listed as your official boyfriend. Official boyfriends don't just ring up and then go back to the police and say, well, I tried, but she told me to get lost and hung up on me.'

It eased the tension a little and both women smiled. Dora said, 'Are you going back today?'

'No. I think I'd be expected to stay at least one night. I'll find a B and B.'

'I'm going to pay you for all this time you've spent on my affairs,' Colette told him. 'I've had the offer of a job.'

'Forget it.' He meant it. The time and the money he'd lost meant nothing against keeping the stubborn bitch alive.

'There's a spare room here,' Dora said. 'That would save the cost of a hotel.'

'I'd not want to put you to any trouble — '

'It'll be no trouble.'

'Yes, you must stay,' Colette added. 'It'll be nice to have some male company.'

Crane thought maybe it was a bit more than that. The nights would still be a difficult time for them, even though there'd be a police presence out there. But an ex-cop actually in the house would be a relief. 'Well, thanks,' he said, 'that's good of you.'

Dora said, 'We eat about half-seven. Salmon steaks. Will that be all right for you?'

'More than all right.' He was hungry after the long drive.

Then the door-bell chimed.

Dora gave a start and jumped to her feet. Crane and Colette glanced uneasily at each other. Door-bells chiming had handed them big trouble in Gargrave. Dora moved the curtain slightly. The bay window would give a view of the front door area.

'Oh, it's only Jenny with a parcel. Must have come when we were out.'

She went off and they heard the short interchange of cheerful voices.

Crane said, 'So you do get out now and then?'

She nodded. 'In Dora's car. Mine's still up north. I'll have to get it shipped down. When I start work Dora's going to drop me and pick me up. We know the police shadow us. We try to make it easy for them.'

'And difficult for Brewer.'

'Maybe he'll pack it in one day.'

Crane knew they both knew he never would.

There was a silence in the hallway now, but Dora hadn't returned. 'She'll be opening it in the kitchen,' Colette said. 'She sent back a cardigan that was the wrong size. That'll be the replacement.'

But Dora came in then. Her features were bloodless. She looked like someone who'd just had major surgery. She stared at them, wide-eyed and trembling. Crane leapt up. 'The parcel?'

'I was *expecting* one!' she cried. 'How do they . . . how *can* they . . . ?'

He ran into the kitchen. The package had been opened on one of the surfaces. It had authentic-seeming labels and looked as if it had come from a mail-order firm. Inside was a black and white photograph of Colette as the blonde she'd been, lying on a carpet in a pale-coloured dress which appeared soaked in

224

blood. Printed on the white border at the bottom were the words: TELL YOUR FRIEND WELCOME BACK.

The glossy photo was laid on top of what had to be the dress itself, a light-green one, covered in what looked to be the identical bloodstains as in the photo.

The women came up behind him, Colette almost as pale as Dora. Crane said, 'You don't want to look at this, Colette.'

'Oh, yes I *do*!' she cried. 'I'm getting used to his pathetic bloody games.'

But she wasn't. Crane knew she never would. She was trembling too, but it was with anger. 'Dora, I'm sorry. I'm really sorry you've had such a shock. I couldn't believe there'd be any more of this bloody nonsense, not now I'm living here openly.'

She grasped the photo, studied it. 'He ... they ... whoever, they've used my face from one of the newspaper pictures taken at the time of the trial.'

Crane nodded. Her face in the photo had a look of frozen anguish that went well with the apparent stabbing and the bloodstains. 'Someone with photographic skills connected your head to someone else's torso, maybe a model's, done up in the bloodstained dress. The stains themselves will have been made with the sort of stuff they use in films.'

'How . . . how did he know I was expecting anything?' Dora said, lips quivering.

'I don't know, Dora.'

He obviously had the house under some kind of surveillance, but Crane wasn't going to tell her that. He'd probably shadowed her when she'd taken the cardigan to be returned to the post office. Then made his usual inspired guesses that a replacement would be on its way back in a few days, and got in first. He'd have delivered the box with the dress and the photo in an authentic-looking van to the neighbour when the two women were out, so as not to arouse the suspicions of any police who might have the house under observation.

'I'll put the frightful thing in the bin!' Dora grabbed hold of the box.

'No, keep it. The police will need to know. It might help.'

They all knew it wouldn't.

'Oh, let's have a drink, Dora!' Colette burst out. 'This is what the sick, shitty bastard *does*. And so what we do is carry on as if nothing's happened. If we show him we simply don't care he might back off.'

She put an arm round the other woman's slender shoulders. Dora still trembled uncontrollably. It was her first experience of the elaborate, perverted stunts Brewer got off on.

There'd be more, going by last weekend. Crane didn't see how a woman as nervy and highly strung as she was would be able to cope for very long with Colette under the same roof.

But her lips were drawing into the thin, determined line he'd seen earlier. Colette now looked like the older of the two: tough, reassuring, able to cope with anything life threw at her. It seemed to Crane that Dora was almost being recharged by the other's determination. Maybe that continual recharging of each other was how they faced it out.

Dora took the box and put it on the floor in a larder. Then she took a bottle of sparkling wine from the fridge. 'Let's have some of this,' she said, in a more controlled voice. 'It'll go with the fish. Would you do the honours, Frank?'

He undid the little wire cage, eased out the cork, poured the foaming wine into three flute-shaped glasses. The booze helped a little. Dora began on the preparation of the food, seasoning the salmon steaks and readying the vegetables. She worked with a kind of relieved efficiency, seeming to draw comfort from life's routine chores.

'We'll sit in the dining-room, shall we?'

'Of course not, Dora. No need to be posh with Frank. He's one of us.'

Dora gave a brief, uncertain smile. It looked to Crane as if all her life she'd been caught between doing what she'd prefer to do and what she felt others expected of her. The kitchen was more than big enough to eat in. And it had an informality he felt they needed.

'The kitchen table's fine, Dora,' he told her. 'I'll take my jacket off if you don't mind.'

They had more drinks while the food cooked, and Dora got Crane to open another bottle for the meal itself. They were almost cheerful when they sat down to eat, or at least pretended to be. Crane wouldn't need to drive again and felt he could let go on the wine a little. He could tell the others were just glad of the release the evening drinks brought from the edgy life they were forced to live. They talked generally, about Colette's new job, about Dora thinking she might take a job too, so that the time didn't hang with Colette out of the house. They talked of going for a drink again with old friends, perhaps one day daring to go to London for a show, or Swanage for a weekend.

The tension was still there, but muted, like the pain that still got through from a headache relieved by aspirin. But it was obvious to Crane the comfort the women drew from each other. Colette lived with the idea of sudden death, but he could sense her delight in being back in what she called the real world. Back with her best friend. Being able to chatter and wear her bright clothes and make the most of her looks.

She didn't eat either with that old self-conscious craving. She ate almost casually, as they talked, as if the talk now meant more than the food. She ate only a single course, though Dora had laid on a dessert and a cheese-board. The days when food and drink had had to make up for all the other things missing in her dreary life were now over. Her life was in top gear again and even the fear and the danger couldn't kill the buzz.

But Crane was still very uneasy about them being alone in the house night after night. They went back in the living-room with the coffee cups when the meal was over. He said to Dora as casually as possible, 'Does your husband know about your current circumstances? Colette living here and so on?'

She nodded, with a faint, crooked smile. 'We keep in touch. It's all quite civilized. I think he'd be prepared to come back . . . if that's what you're thinking. Not to . . . live together any more. Just to be around, lend moral support. But neither of us really want it.'

She sipped coffee and gazed out on to the lane, quiet now in the gathering dusk with all

229

the commuter traffic gone. 'There's no one else involved. He said there isn't and I believe him. It was just . . . well, Tony being killed. Men react differently when something like that happens. I never realized. Maybe I'm generalizing. We had a good life: dinners out, theatres, weekends away. He was knocked sideways by the killing, of course, but he couldn't cope with the changes. The grief. Nothing in our lives ever being the same again.'

She shrugged, glanced at Colette. 'Women never stop grieving, I suppose. I had Tony, spent all those early years with him. He was, well, just part of me, and because he was an only child a very big part. I pined. I knew I could never get over it, but I lived with it. I carried on. Harry couldn't. And he couldn't live with my unhappiness. His instinct, in the end, seemed to be to stuff it all in a corner of his mind and close a door on it. And then he wanted life to go on as before. He couldn't do with any more reminders of what had happened, and he saw them in me every day. It seemed the only way he could deal with it was to break away and make a completely new life for himself . . . '

The sad words faded into a lengthy silence. It was abruptly broken by the door-bell chiming again.

13

Dora's cup and saucer rattled. She put them down on a small table and went to peep round the curtain again. 'It's . . . it's a man,' she said, in a low voice. 'It's no one I recognize.'

'Look through the spy-glass, Colette,' Crane told her. 'If he means nothing to you I'll answer it and keep the chain on.'

They went in the hall and she put an eye to the little glass. Then she stepped back, leaned against the wall, closed her eyes and sighed. 'Christ, not *him*! That's all I need!'

'Him?'

'Robert. Ring any bells? That reptile my mother had the bad luck to marry.'

'What's he doing *here*?' Dora said, in a high voice.

'One guess.'

The door-bell chimed a second time. Crane said, 'Do we let him in?'

She sighed again. 'Knowing that bastard he'll not go away till we do. You can't believe the persistence of the man. And the brass neck.'

He opened the door. The man outside gave

him a brief hostile glance before looking past him to Colette. '*Colette!*' he cried. 'We've been worried *sick*. Oh, just to see you again . . . '

He was about five-ten, well built and wearing a pale-blue lightweight suit, a blue shirt and a grey tie. He had fleshy lips, eyes that gave an impression of intensity and fair hair that covered his head in dense, almost negroid curls. He couldn't take his eyes off her. They moved from her face to her body in the bright clothes, then back to her face again. It was clear to Crane he'd never managed to get over her since he'd first moved in with her mother.

'I suppose you'd better come in,' Colette said. It was a voice that could freeze alcohol.

He lunged through the door, ready to take her in his arms, maybe even to kiss her. She slipped deftly out of range, looking as if she'd had a lot of practice. 'This is my stepfather,' she said pointedly. 'Robert Marshall.' She didn't give Marshall their names.

'Do come through, Mr Marshall,' Dora said, ever polite.

'Thank you, ma'am.' He glanced at Crane again, still hostile. 'Colette, it's been so *long*! You can't begin to know how much we've missed you.'

'How did you know I was here?'

'It's been in the papers, about you leaving that witness protection business. They said you were back in Woking. I knew you'd be here. The minute I read it I had to make sure you were all right.'

'Well, I'm fine, Robert, just fine, as you can see. So we'll not keep you.'

'Oh, Colette . . . ' He gave a pained smile. 'Always one for the jokes.'

'Does Mum know you're here?'

'Well, of course — '

'Why not bring her with you then?'

'I'm going to,' he said, in a hurt voice, 'but I was along this way with my job. I just felt I had to try and see you.'

'How is Mum?'

'She's fine, just fine,' he said briskly, but Crane caught the note of indifference. 'Missing you terribly, of course. You must come home soon, Col. I could take you back tonight, spend the weekend with us.'

'I'd prefer Mum to come here, if she feels up to it. On her own.'

'It wouldn't be the same, love. You need to be with your family, in your own home. Your mum, Oliver, me . . . in fact, why not live with us permanently, now you've decided to leave that frightful programme? Your mum would love to have you back, especially with Oliver talking of moving in with his girlfriend.'

'I'm sure you'd love that too, Robert,' she said flatly. 'It'd be just like old times, yes, when you used to burst in my room when I was half-dressed and try to paw me about. With Oliver gone you'd only need to make sure Mum was on her way to Waitrose.'

His healthy colour deepened. He'd not thought she'd bring up his old habits in front of strangers. He gave Crane and Dora an embarrassed glance. Dora looked pained but still attentively polite, as if not quite sure what was expected of her, as usual. 'Can we speak in private, Col? I care about you, that's why I want you to come home, but it's mainly because your mother misses you so much. I know I gave the wrong impression now and then in the past, but — '

'It wasn't an impression. You burst in on me when I was half-dressed when you'd not been married two months, and then you tried to blackmail me into sleeping with you.'

He'd gone even redder. Looked badly done to. Crane sensed he'd recycled his memories of what had actually happened and had now convinced himself his version was the true one. He wasn't surprised, it was a convenient mindset he'd begun to see in Ted Benson.

'Please, Colette, a word in private.'

'No. Dora and Frank are my closest friends

234

and I have no secrets from them. They've given me *genuine* help in my trouble. I've had a lot on my mind and the one thing I can do without is having to listen to an arsehole like you rewriting history.'

Marshall gave Crane a hard, angry stare. It looked to Crane he could just about cope with being called an arsehole in front of them, but not that he was one of her closest friends. He gave him a harder stare back, a skill he'd honed over many years. The kid had seen her boyfriend killed, had psyched herself up to giving evidence, and there was a nutter out there wanting to kill her. And Marshall's main reaction seemed to be how soon he could begin trying to talk her into taking her kit off again.

'I know you've had a bad time,' he said finally, 'and I know you're still at risk. But if you'll come home I'll take care of you. Believe me, they'd have to kill me before they could get near you.'

His voice was thick with emotion. Crane found himself believing him. He gave a powerful impression of a man so deeply infatuated that if anything should happen to her he'd barely have any reason to go on living. He'd rarely seen a man in such a state of longing. Shallow breathing, dilated pupils, hands that continually half-moved towards her, as if he could barely restrain himself from touching her.

In the end he couldn't help pitying the poor sod. He'd married her mother in good faith, that was obvious, but what he'd felt for Colette was something else. It was the kind of attraction that only seemed to hit you once in a lifetime, if at all, and was just about impossible to shake off. It was what the French called the *coup de foudre* and Crane had been there.

They sat in silence, Crane and Colette back on the long sofa, Dora and Marshall in armchairs. Then Colette gave Marshall a faint, near-kindly smile. 'I miss them terribly, Robert, but it's best if Mum's kept away from all this business with the Brewers, however carefully you looked after us. I'm staying with Dora indefinitely. We need each other and we understand the situation. It doesn't make too much sense to outsiders.'

'Look, Colette — '

'Forget about me and just look after Mum. You married her and you make her happy. If I ever came back we both know what it would mean. We do, don't we?'

He looked from her to Crane. 'This your new boyfriend?' he said scornfully. 'This the best you can do, last thing left in the bran tub?'

'I'm a private investigator, Mr Marshall,' Crane said evenly. 'I've done some work for Colette. In that time I've come to admire her spirit and her courage. I'm exactly what she says I am, just a friend she can rely on. The man she can't get over is the man Donny Brewer murdered. She really can do without further complications in her life right now.'

'You from the north?'

'I'll be going back there over the weekend.'

'You're going to leave two women on their own with a hired gun on the loose! She'd be a hundred times safer with her mother and me. And this other lady, Dora, would be safer without her being here.'

'They've gone into all that and they've chosen to be together. And the police have the house under surveillance. It's not as safe as the programme, but if there's one thing the police can't afford it's to let anything happen to either of them.'

'It must be difficult to understand, Mr Marshall,' Dora said, in her polite way. 'It's because we both loved him so much, my son. We *are* frightened, such a lot of the time, but we can face it if we're together.'

She also had flushed slightly. Colette gave her a warm smile. But her words had had little effect on Marshall, who was now glancing impatiently at his watch.

'It's getting late for me to drive all the way back to Kent. Could I stay here tonight, Dora? I'd be very grateful.'

'No, you bloody *can't!*' Colette cried. 'It was your idea to come here pestering me. How you get back is your affair.'

'And I'm afraid Frank's sleeping in the spare,' Dora added. She sounded slightly regretful, as if feeling she had to soften the effect of Colette's harshness.

'I'll kip down on the sofa, no problem,' he said. 'All I'd need is a spare duvet.'

Crane wondered what he sold for a living, houses or insurance, to be so quick on his feet.

'You're not sleeping *anywhere* in this house, Robert,' Colette snapped. 'Or the garden shed. You've gawped at my tits once by bursting in on me. Well, that was once too many and I wasn't born yesterday.'

He looked hurt again, his eyes were suddenly wistful. Crane thought maybe he'd never got it off his mind, the single glimpse he'd had of her, naked from the waist up.

'There's the Dutch,' Dora told him solicitously, 'across the canal on Woodham Road. It's a good B and B and they might have a vacancy. I could ring, if you like.'

He sighed heavily. 'Please don't bother, Dora. I'll sort something out,' he said, glancing at Crane. But Crane knew driving to Kent would be no problem at this time of night, with the pressure off the Orbital. He wanted to stay to buy time, to find a way of talking to her in private. But he wasn't going to get it. Crane could detect all the signs of a powerful inner struggle.

Finally, even redder in the face, he said, 'Look, Col, I really am very sorry about . . . Tony. How unhappy you've been. I mean it. But . . . but look, you really do need someone to look after you properly and — '

'Robert.' She cut him off, on a warning note.

'I'll give you a good life,' he said quickly. 'I make a good living. I could buy you a nice house, holidays, a decent car and . . . well, if you wanted children one day, that wouldn't be a problem.'

She gave him a blank, open-mouthed stare. 'What are you burbling about!' she cried. 'You're married to *Mum*!'

'I'll sort it out. Tell her I can't go on living a lie. Tell her I can't help it, I'm just crazy about you and always will be. I'll make it right financially. The house is hers anyway, but I'll make her an allowance — '

'Stop, stop, for Christ's sake *stop*!' she screamed. 'Do you ever listen? I don't know what goes on in your head, but what makes you think I'd *ever* want to make do with you? It's not just that you married Mum, it's because you never got inside a hundred miles of turning me on. And do you know what it is, this repulsive, disgusting offer, when I knew a man like Tony Powell, it's a fucking *insult*! Now go. Just *go*!'

She shook with rage. Her eyes glistened with tears and she was almost gasping for breath. It seemed to Crane that after an outburst like that even Marshall, with his elephant hide, would have been able to take it as a no. But he was wrong.

'Look,' he said, in a low gentle voice, 'I know what a lousy time you've had, what with the trial and then having to hide yourself up north all these months. That's why I want to make it up to you. Think it over, Col, that's all I ask. I know I could make you happy one day, if you'd give it a chance. I've . . . I've got enough love for both of us, you see.'

'Oh God, Frank,' she almost whispered, brushing her eyes with the back of her hand. 'Is this really happening? I don't have nightmares this bad. Will you *please* get this lunatic away from me.'

Crane got up. 'You heard her, Marshall, on your feet. You couldn't have upset her more if you'd tried.'

The other man jumped up angrily. 'You

240

watch your mouth, detective, if you don't want a bunch of fives. This is sod-all to do with you; it's between me and her. I go when I'm good and ready. Understood?'

'Really, Mr Marshall, I do think it's for the best,' Dora said, even her politeness under strain. 'You must see how very badly you've upset her.'

'Someone did once give me a bunch of fives,' Crane told him calmly, 'but he'd have made two of you.'

Both standing, Crane had several inches on him. He was broader and obviously stronger. He grasped Marshall firmly by the arm, who began to struggle but thought better of it.

'I'm going to leave you with this thought, Marshall. Colette doesn't want to see you again, not ever. Now if you cause her any more aggro there will be a bunch of fives on the go and believe me, it won't be yours.'

He marched him into the hall, but halfway along Marshall suddenly yanked him to a halt and shouted, 'Colette, I love you! I can't do anything about it. Please don't give up on me, just let me see you now and then. I'll always be there for you, whether you want me or not. And I'll never let *anyone* harm you . . . '

He walked to the door then of his own accord. Crane opened it. 'Look, mate,' he said, 'I can see it's the real thing. Believe me,

I know. But what I've had to learn is that it's no good if they don't want you. You're going to have to settle for the mother.'

Marshall smoothed the lapels of his expensive jacket, straightened his tie, ran a hand through his tight curls. He glanced at Crane absently. Crane knew he never would settle for the mother. He was the compulsive type who never settled for anything less than what he'd set his mind on. A Mercedes was parked in front of the house.

'If anything should happen to that woman, mister,' he said, in a low, rasping voice, 'the swine who did it'll wish he'd never been born.'

★ ★ ★

Crane went back in the living-room. Dora sat with an arm round Colette, comforting her. Colette, still moist-eyed, looked up with a wan smile. 'Thank God you were here. I don't know how I'd ever have got shot of him.'

He nodded. 'He's in a real state about you. Can't help feeling a bit sorry for him. I know it doesn't excuse anything.'

'I just wish he'd never laid eyes on me. He'd have been so much happier. I really liked him an awful lot at first. He can be very funny, good company. You know, salesman's gift of the gab. And he was so good for Mum. Still is, I hope. As long as he's around I think that's all that matters to her.'

'I . . . feel rather sorry for him too,' Dora said hesitantly. 'I'm sure he must have fallen for you for the same reason Tony did. Because you're full of life and everything seems better when you're around.'

'Oh, Dora . . .'

'I know he upset you terribly, but he seems such a caring person beneath it all. I'm sure he'd be absolutely reliable if you ever did go back home and were in danger. That's such a good thing in a man.'

Crane caught the wistful note in her voice. He wondered if she hadn't taken quite a shine to Robert Marshall for all his brashness. It could be she thought he wasn't the type who'd leg it when there was a crisis. Unlike Harry, who looked to have been a blue-skies man.

Dora said, 'I really should have offered the poor man a drink, but everything happened so quickly. Will you have a brandy, Frank?'

'A small one would be nice.'

'Let's all have one, Dora.'

'We often play cards in the evening,' Dora told him, 'but we can watch the telly if you'd rather.'

'Please do whatever you normally do. I'll go along with it.'

'Let's make it cards then. What do you suggest?'

'Have you tried Poker?'

The women looked at each other, shook their heads. They moved to the dining-table in another clean and airy room, with wall-lights in the shape of gas-lamps, seascapes, an antique sideboard, and a corner cupboard filled with china and glass. Crane began to teach them the game, with its many variations, its flushes, full houses, runs and pairs. It was an absorbing way of occupying their minds at what had to be the worst time of day, the darkness and silence of night-time. The women gave the cards total concentration, quickly mastered the hands and the rules, and were finally playing a fast mean game, no corner given, with counters given a value of ten pence each. For a time they were both able to forget themselves and their situation.

Dora was soon in the lead. She had judgement and luck, and the counters began to mount on her side of the table. Maybe she'd have lost it all, gambling the lot on a hand she thought couldn't lose, but they never reached that stage.

Because the door-bell chimed for a third time that day.

14

'I'll go,' Crane said, holding up a hand in a calming gesture. 'And I'll be very careful.'

'Who can it possibly be at this time of night?' Dora said. Her hand had jerked when the bell sounded and her pile of counters had scattered across the table.

Crane moved into the hall, put on the light. There were panels of opaque glass each side of the door which threw light on to the door area. He put an eye to the viewing glass. He could make out fair hair, a well-knit body in a dark jerkin and a navy turtle-neck sweater. The man produced what looked to be a warrant card and held it to the glass. Crane opened the door a crack, on the chain.

'I can understand your caution, Mr Crane. The name's Luke Tetley and I'm a detective sergeant with the local force.' He continued to hold up his warrant card until satisfied it had been checked out. 'Can we have a word?'

'You seem to know about me.'

The other smiled faintly. 'We all know about you, sir; we're in constant touch with the people up north. You're here to talk

Colette Jennings into going back into witness protection.'

'And not having much luck, to be honest.'

'Stick with it. We're all sorry for the kid, but we're one worried bunch of coppers.'

'Me too. I've been trying to get the older woman on my side. So far she's being as stubborn as Colette.'

'We need to talk, Mr Crane, preferably not on the doorstep or in front of the women. You'll understand when I've explained. Do you want to sit in the car? I'm with a colleague but he's gone for the take-away. Don't worry, there are four of us out there, all highly trained. Very highly trained.'

Crane nodded, relieved but still uneasy. Glad of the strength of numbers, but that meant the police were taking the threat to her life very, very seriously.

'Hold on. I'll just let them know where I'll be. Come in.'

'I'll stay in the hall. I know they've had it up to here with policemen. And relock this door, would you, just to be on the safe side.'

It added to Crane's anxiety, but he did as asked. Then left him there and went back in the dining-room. They sat exactly as he'd left them, like waxworks.

'Police,' he told them. 'Bloke called Tetley. He wants to talk to me and we're going to sit

246

in his car.' He lowered his voice. 'You can guess what he wants, and I'm having to say I'm pulling all the stops out to get Colette back in the programme. Don't answer the door to anyone till I'm back. I'll ring the bell three times.'

They nodded without a word, both looking relieved. He went back to where Tetley stood on the doormat, studying a barometer. He was a good-looking man, his hair wavy and thick, blue-eyed, the features bluntish and strong, and standing just below six foot at a guess, but his lean frame making him seem taller. 'It's rising, the glass,' he said. 'Let's hope that means a decent clear day tomorrow.'

He spoke as if this was meant to be significant but didn't say why. They went out to his motor, a few yards down from the house on a road now fairly clear of parked cars. They got in a two-litre Volvo that smelt of onion-flavoured crisps, cigarettes, and the little coloured bobbles of air-freshener some people hung from the rear-view mirror. It was the authentic smell of police surveillance.

'All right, Mr Crane. Mind if I call you Frank?'

'I'd prefer it.'

'I'm Luke, as you know. How long do you aim to be staying at Mrs Powell's?'

'I was hoping to go back tomorrow, but I'm flexible till Sunday.'

'They tell me you're an ex-cop.'

'They're right.'

'It helps. You'll know how we tend to operate.'

'I've given it all I've got, Luke, trying to talk her back in the programme, but she's dead against it. Crazy, I know.'

'So I've gathered,' he said, with a heavy sigh. He gazed along the quiet road. It was fully dark now, the light of a street-lamp shining on his mop of hair and outlining the firm set of his mouth and chin. Crane could sense the competence. 'Look, Frank, we've got reliable info Lenny Brewer is ready to go for it. We have a snout or two inside Donny's nick we can trust. The word is he's spitting feathers about Lenny pissing about. You know, the things he's done to scare the shit out of the kid. The Leeds people told us the kind of tricks he was pulling when you were on the run in Yorkshire.'

'There's one trick you don't know about yet,' Crane said. He told him about the photograph and the stained dress.

'Sadistic bastard.' Luke gave a grim smile. 'That's what all the trouble's been about. Donny's got an evil temper on him he never could control, but at least he's a normal villain, if you know what I mean, with normal reactions. He just wants Colette seeing to because she put him inside. He can't be doing with all this bent stuff Lenny gets off on: wreaths and bloodstained dresses, beaten up DCs. He also thinks Lenny's buggered about so much he might have spoilt his chances of a clean hit on Colette, now he's got so many of us on the go. He could have a point. They had a bust-up, according to our source, with Donny telling Lenny to stop fucking about and get the job *done*. Fast, like inside a week. And her so exposed now the postman could take her out. And when Donny gets really heavy even Lenny jumps because Donny still controls all the funny money the boys are sitting on.'

Crane said, 'You say Donny thinks he might have spoilt his chances . . . '

Tetley began to look moody. 'It's a big might. Well, you know about Lenny's early background: Para, mercenary, all that shit. One of the guys who ran around with him in Africa, he told us you could have a piece of flat terrain, no trees, no cover of any kind, but Lenny'd find a way of losing himself in there somehow. But maybe, just maybe, for the first time in his life he's overplayed his hand. Let's hope to Christ he has.'

He turned back to Crane, eyes glinting, mouth a hard line. 'I've been trying to nail that arsehole for twelve months, Frank. We've had three recent killings on Donny's patch. Two were gangland business we couldn't give a fiddler's fuck about, saved us a job. The other was a gilt-edged witness we were hoping would help us take the lid off Donny's entire set-up. It covers the lot: drugs, toms, illegals, illegals they can use as toms, you name it, even though he'd come down here to launder into straight operations. That witness was a kid no older than Colette. Fell from a multistorey car-park. It *looked* like an accident, and the coroner had to log it as one in the end, but we knew it was Lenny. He'd not even need to touch her. All he'd need to do was come towards her with that sick, evil stare of his and she'd be so scared she'd try to get away from him any way she could. Her name was Lucy Mailer. I've never forgotten her and I never will.'

Crane knew what he was saying. He'd been there himself, could almost feel his pain. The other man breathed deeply as if to calm himself. 'All right,' he muttered, 'it was personal. I'm not proud of myself. I'm married, kids. I kicked off just feeling sorry for her, ended up knowing that if I wasn't careful I'd be adding to the divorce statistics.

'She was very pretty, very naive and very vulnerable. She fell for one of the Brewer people. Had no real idea what he did at first. Thought he was one of the City lads, making a nice wedge in the square mile. He was good-looking, a big spender, liked to show off. And couldn't keep his trap shut. She was naive, as I said, but she cottoned in the end. And by the time he'd got his eye on another piece of totty she knew as much about the rackets as he did. Names, places, *modus operandi*, the works. And was persuaded to talk about it. By me.'

He breathed in again. 'Well, that's another story. And I wish I could feel glad my marriage is back on track. I'll tell you this, if I could ever get near Lenny Brewer and there was no one around to see or hear anything I'd put the twisted sod down myself. I'd not think twice about it and I'd think I'd done society a fucking good turn. You didn't hear that.'

But Crane had been there too, and knew at first hand what could goad a policeman to take a short cut. Emotion seemed to thicken the atmosphere like humidity, a hatred Tetley looked to live with all his waking life. But Tetley's bitterness had to be a big plus when they were up against a man as cunning as Brewer. With Tetley on the case he felt

251

hopeful for the first time of her chances of staying alive.

'I have another snout,' Tetley said, more collected now. 'He hangs out with the Brewer people. Kind of a gangster groupie, know what I mean? He's not one of them, but they let him clean the cars, run errands, earn a few sovs on a dog-race they've fixed, that sort of stuff. They tell him next to sod-all, but one thing he did pick up on is that they're being very tight-lipped about what they're doing tomorrow. That's unusual.

'Know what I think? I think Lenny's aiming to put on a final show this weekend and finish Colette off. That way both Brewers get their satisfaction: Lenny has his last nasty kicks and Donny sees his contract settled.'

Crane watched him in silence.

'This is where I'd like you to come in, Frank, and it's why I didn't want the women involved. You probably won't know Woking too well, but in the middle of the shopping centre there's an open square. There's a big complex off it called The Peacocks and another called Wolsey Place. We're talking M & S, dress-shops, Sainsbury's and jewellers, right. The Peacocks is the most elaborate, it has an atrium and glass-sided lifts and cafés on the ground floor. Between The Peacocks and Wolsey Place there's also a more

252

traditional market with stalls, called Peacock Walk. You know, ties and hankies, cheap CDs, watches, tat. On Saturday that square's humming, and tomorrow's even more of a razzmatazz day. Kids singing for charity, clowns, balloons, dodgems, the full monty.'

He brought his face a little closer to Crane's. 'It's the only chance we've got, Frank. Let's assume Brewer is aiming to pull something off tomorrow, but he doesn't know what Colette and Dora are aiming to do, obviously. But that gives Lenny no grief because he's master-class at playing it by ear.

'But what if *we* called the shots on the venue? What if we arranged for you and the women to stroll along to the square? We'd watch you every foot of the way there and we'd have our people covering you. From every angle.'

'You don't seriously believe Brewer would try anything on in the middle of a *crowd!*'

'That's exactly what I'm saying. A Brewer spectacular. You've been a cop; you know how people react when something dramatic happens in a crowded place. Some joker sets a firework off, say, or a brawl breaks out or a knife gets pulled. It's just total confusion and women yelping and people not wanting to get involved. They don't see what's happening in front of their eyes correctly.'

Crane shook his head. 'A killing in a crowded place? He couldn't *hope* to get away.'

'We're talking Lenny Brewer, Frank,' Tetley said softly. 'And he'd know exactly how to leg it. He'd have some of his people causing a diversion, he'd see to Colette, and he'd be off on his toes through The Peacocks. He knows how to wear clothes and disguises he can dump on the run. There's a way through The Peacocks to the car-park and he'd have a wheelman waiting. He'd have other people ready to swear he was a hundred miles away when it was all happening.'

He was silent for a few seconds. 'But he couldn't try any of that, Frank, unless Colette was already there.'

'And you want me to get her there.'

'Tell them it would cheer them up to see the festivities. You'll be with them, a big bloke they can trust, and you'll say they're bound to be safe in a crowd. It's the accepted wisdom, Christ knows why. Meantime *we'll* be there, dressed like everyone else: tops, jeans, T-shirts, sports coats. There'll be a lot of us and we'll be within yards of you all the time. But we *have* to see that knife, Frank, or that gun, or whatever other weapon he's got down his trouser-leg. The second we've got eye-ball on the weapon we drop him like a bag of cement.'

'I don't know, Luke,' Crane said warily. 'What if he dropped her before you could react? We're talking Lenny Brewer; your words. You'd probably nail him but the kid could be dead.'

Tetley nodded, tapped Crane's knee. 'That's why the decision has to be yours. And it's a toughie. But we'll have handpicked people in place. We'll have the surrounding buildings covered. There's a church, a bank, a library, the stock floors of the shops. We'll have people in every one of them with the powerful bins, always in contact with the rest of us.'

It was Crane's turn to gaze in silence along the road. Tetley sat patient and still. He'd learnt how to keep his energy intact for possible action. Crane could see it his way. It had to be the best chance they were ever going to get to flush him from his usual deep cover. And there was an outside chance Colette would be killed however carefully they guarded her. On the other hand her chances of staying alive outside the programme were minimal. But if she was killed in the square they'd be virtually certain to drop Brewer. Put him up for a murder they could prove to make up for the ones they couldn't. To police minds he knew they'd be making the very best of an incredibly complicated situation. Ends justifying dodgy means. Crane knew he'd be thinking the same way, had he not got to know Colette.

'Frank . . . ?'

Crane sighed. 'Just make absolutely sure the cavalry's in place and some bugger's there the second anyone gets inside a yard of her, even if it's a Little Sister of the Poor.'

Luke gave his grim smile. '*Especially* if it's a Little Sister of the Poor. Good man!'

'It sounds as if you've already set things up.'

'We brainstormed, ran it past the big people. We've got bodies on standby, pending me getting your agreement. We sold it as a package. If we can nobble Lenny for attempted murder the whole Donny Brewer set — up begins to fall apart, with the brains and the discipline gone. We've seen it happen before. We turn the heat on the rest of the goons and in the end they decide they'll have a better life either going straight or fucking off.'

Crane smiled wryly. He knew the police, knew they'd not have risked such a costly operation unless they could be convinced there was more to be gained than just keeping a woman alive who was getting to be a monumental pain in the arse.

'You're sure Brewer will show?'

'His people never lose track of the two women. You must know that. The second they tell him you're all leaving the house together he'll make his plans on the hoof. He'll be there. Look at me, Dad, I took her out with half Woking looking on.'

'It's something I've never been able to work out,' Crane said. 'Just how they found the time to watch Dora's house so closely. How did they pick up on me, right at the start, when I came down here trying to find out why Dora had gone missing? I was pretending to be a council officer and could have been one for all they knew.'

'That bugged me a lot. And then one of our bright young DCs made the connection. The Brewers are legally in the property business, yes, buy-to-lets, all that stuff. Well, what if they owned a property on Eastern Lane? And they *do*. It's across the road, diagonally to our left of where I'm parked. They rent it out on short leases to young execs who need to work in the Smoke for a few months. Only they've not rented it out since Donny went inside. They've been using the front bedroom as an office and they've got a bloke in there actually working, sometimes two. We reckon it's some bent accountant who plans laundering scams and moves the money around off-shore. Only he can combine the work with keeping an eye on Dora's place. Anyone calls there, anyone at all, apart from the postman, the meter-readers and the window-cleaner, he reports back to the main office, someone checks it out, and if it looks tasty tells Lenny. Because Lenny must have been certain the only chance he had of getting through to Colette was by someone, one day, coming down here on a mission.'

'So *that's* it.' Crane sat back in his seat. 'I beat my brains to a pulp trying to figure that one.'

'Another aspect of Lenny's cunning, my friend. He knows just how close the women have always been. But tomorrow, if it's anything to do with me, could be the day of reckoning.'

Crane glanced at his watch. 'This numbers-man. He'll be there now?'

The other shook his head. 'They've knocked off the night-shift, now that Colette's back living with Dora. They just concentrate on what the women do during the day. They know they're too scared yet to go out at night.'

'You've put a lot of work and thought into this.'

'Colette's been a bloody fool, Frank. We both know it. But when I heard the way she'd fooled everyone up north, in the blonde wig and the fancy clothes, well, I had to admit the kid had nerve and guts. We'll do every mortal thing we can to keep her in one piece. And with any luck put Brewer in Belmarsh with his old man. Would that make my fucking day . . . '

'All right, Luke. I'll aim to get them there mid-morning.'

'That would be ideal. And thanks. I knew we could rely on you. And this briefing never happened, right? You'll be in the square completely by chance. Try not to contact me beforehand but if you have to, ring me on this mobile number.' He passed Crane a slip of paper with the number written on. 'No one, but no one must know anything of this outside a handpicked team of people I can trust. And whatever the result I'll personally make sure the police up north know about the valuable co-operation you've given us.'

He held out his hand and gave Crane's a firm dry shake. 'Well,' Crane said, 'best of luck.'

'I *feel* lucky about this one. It's not always the case, believe me. One last thing. Whatever gives tomorrow around Colette don't get involved yourself, otherwise you might get in the way of people expert in this kind of set-up. OK?'

Crane nodded. But it might not be easy keeping his instincts under that kind of control.

★ ★ ★

The women sat over the abandoned hands of cards, talking quietly.

Colette said, 'What was it all about, Frank?'

'The same old CD. They simply haven't the resources to keep on guarding you like this indefinitely.'

'Poor Frank.' She touched his hand. 'Another bollocking?'

'I did tell him not to shoot the messenger if I'd brought the wrong message, but it got me nowhere.'

Dora said, 'We're putting you to such a lot of trouble.'

'I can handle it, Dora, don't worry. Now, where were we with our game? Maybe we'd better start with fresh cards.'

'Wouldn't you rather watch television?'

'No, I'm anxious to get my hands on that pile of counters of yours.'

But what he needed was to occupy his mind as much as they did. Tomorrow morning hung over him now. He wished he could talk to them about it. Share the strain and the persistent guilt of what he might be leading them into. But if he told them they'd be too scared to go. They had to walk on to that square in as relaxed a way as everyone else, two women out to see the festivities and do a little shopping. It was vital Brewer with his hair-trigger instincts, didn't sense a set-up.

So they played on for another hour or so. Colette ended up with the most counters, as Dora made several unwise decisions. Crane hoped to God it was a good omen. They all made for bed then. Crane said goodnight to them, then checked the doors, the window-locks and the intruder alarm. He washed and cleaned his teeth in the downstairs cloak-room, made his way to the third bedroom. There was the VDU, modem and printer of a personal computer in there, set up on a little desk, a three-quarter bed, a fitted wardrobe and a bookcase filled with text-books on accounting methods and tax-laws. Harry had made the spare double as a study, in line with half of middle-class Britain. Before he'd legged it, because it had to be ring-fenced, the grief and a life that had stopped being fun.

He stripped to his boxers. He had a small case that went everywhere with him that held a change of linen and a toilet bag. He was swinging himself into bed when he heard the slightest tap on the door. Colette slipped inside, her hair brushed out and wearing a striped pink and white nightdress with an embroidered yoke.

'How about another nice cuddle?'

'What about Dora?'

'She's taken a sleeping pill since leaving the clinic. I watched her take it and when I glanced in she was hard and fast.'

He dowsed the bedside lamp and heard once again the whisper of fabric as she took off the nightdress. She slipped into bed with him, smelling of toothpaste and scented soap. 'I like small beds,' she murmured. 'Very cosy.'

He'd not thought he'd be sleeping with her again. Not under Dora's roof, the house where she'd met her murdered lover. It was a nice surprise in a life that didn't hold too many. Maybe they'd both needed the release of sex. She'd been out of the programme a week and living in fear. He was worried about what tomorrow might bring. He could lose himself for a time in the curves and softness of the body he'd got to know, the full breasts and buttocks, the softer flesh of the inner thighs. But her body was beginning to feel tauter. Maybe she was already beginning to fine down from the days of comfort eating. She enjoyed sex and she was good at it. They made the most of each other in the silent darkness, but still didn't kiss, both accepting it was nothing to do with love, only affection.

They finally lay back. 'Dora doesn't expect me to live like the parish spinster, you know,' she said quietly, in her husky voice, 'because of Tony. She *wants* me to find someone some day, she often says so. But you're right, she'd not like to think of me in bed with you in her own house.' She sighed. 'I like you, Frank, an awful lot. Maybe it's a pity we don't, you know . . . '

'Maybe if I'd met you before you and Tony.'

'And before you and . . . whoever . . . '

She knew. Some women could always tell. He felt it was like a concealed scar they could only pick up on when they were in bed with you and touched naked flesh.

'It's a long, complicated story.'

'She's not . . . dead too?'

'She might as well be. She'll not be back.'

'There's only one who really counts. I never used to believe it when I was playing the field. But there is, and whichever way you wrap it up all it'll ever be with the others is making do.'

They didn't speak again, and then her regular breathing told him she was asleep. A healthy sex-session had been her sleeping-pill.

Crane thought it ironic that Robert would have changed his entire life for what she'd been so willing to share with him. Poor guy. He'd seemed almost deranged. He had to be if he could convince himself he'd ever be a match for the likes of Lenny Brewer.

Crane was normally a good sleeper, but the guilt persisted and kept him awake. He'd enjoyed the sex with her, but in the morning he'd be putting her in the firing-line. The body he'd made the most of tonight might tomorrow be lying on a slab.

Tetley had told him they'd be checking out the buildings lining the square, but what if Brewer dressed himself as a workman and managed to get on the roof? What if he picked her off in the crowd then legged it down a fire escape, discarding overalls as he went, so that now he wore a quiet suit and glasses and maybe a little beard, and could have been a librarian or a store manager?

Or maybe he'd come in close, one of the nice old men he did so well, with wrinkles and wire-rimmed glasses, and wearing an old suit-jacket over flannel trousers. And maybe he'd have a small, silenced gun, and you'd hardly see or hear him getting off the rounds, and no one would know he'd been there till Colette collapsed dying, the sweet-smelling kid who now lay at his side. And the little old man would have blended into the background. No problem for a man who'd been able to lose himself in terrain where there was barely enough cover to conceal a snake.

He could call it off. Ring Tetley and tell him he'd decided it was just too dangerous, however well trained his team were. But Brewer would get her in the end. He was one focused killer. He'd had Dora's house on permanent watch from the house across the way ever since they'd hidden Colette in West Yorkshire. If he called it off tomorrow it would only delay Brewer, not stop him. And next time the police wouldn't be out in force, with the hardware.

He finally fell into a sleep so disturbed he felt he was still awake. Towards morning he dreamt he was in Trafalgar Square, with its fountains and tourists. He was running diagonally across it from the St Martin's Place end, dodging around knots of people. In the middle of the square a dense crowd formed a shocked circle. He clawed his way to its centre, shouted at by people he pushed roughly aside. She lay in the middle, on her back, in the striped nightdress, which was now soaked in blood. Her amber eyes had the opaque glaze of a dead rabbit. As he watched, a maggot began to wriggle from the corner of her pale lips.

He came to with a jolt, heart beating like a two-stroke engine. She lay at his side, smiling faintly in her sleep, her hand resting on his belly. He eased himself out of bed. Her eyes began to open slowly and she looked at him oddly. He remembered it too well, the day she'd simply not known who he was. This was similar but not the same. Maybe she'd been smiling in her sleep because she was dreaming she was with Tony again, had reached out and touched what had to be his body. To wake up and find it wasn't Tony, just Crane.

'Hi there,' he said, with a stab at sounding cheerful.

'Hello, Frank.' He couldn't miss the note of disillusion.

She hunched herself up against the padded headboard. He'd thought the nights would be the worst time for the women, but maybe the early mornings had the edge. Many, many people woke up not ready to face life, but that didn't begin to compare to Colette's plight, who woke knowing Tony would never be back and that the murderer's son was committed to killing her, too.

She was gutsy and spirited, and maybe when she was up and about and the blood sugar started to kick in she'd begin to feel more her stubborn self. But in the first minutes of a new day she looked scared and defenceless. Her nakedness underlined it.

He put his arms around her. She clung to him. He felt the warmth of tears against his skin. He held her for minutes, stroking her tousled hair. Finally, her voice uneven, she said, 'I'd better go to my room before Dora wakes. I'm so glad you're here. Please stay till tomorrow . . .'

He went in the bathroom, showered, dressed and went down to make coffee. He sipped it, looking through the kitchen window at the lengthy back garden with its carefully cut lawn and its patio, its umbrellaed table and chairs and its ornamental trees: cherry, maple and laburnum. He listened to the 'Today' programme, with its news updates, interviews and weather forecast. A day of sunlight and clear skies was promised for the south-east, as Tetley had hoped. Crane couldn't shake off his uneasiness, the persistent picture of three people setting out for the centre and only two coming back.

The women came down together, showered, combed and wearing crisp summer dresses. 'I'm sure you must be hungry, Frank,' Dora said, in her usual solicitous way, 'I hope we've not made you wait too long. What will you have, bacon and egg?'

267

'Nothing, Dora, thanks all the same.'

'Are you sure? Harry always liked a cooked breakfast.'

'Coffee's fine.'

'Well, if you're sure,' she said dubiously. 'Let me make some fresh then.'

He wondered if Harry thought he'd ever find anyone who'd look after him as she'd done. Maybe he woke these mornings longing to be back, but with the old Dora, not the one who lived with the ghost of their dead son.

They all sat together at the kitchen table, Colette just having toast and tea in place of the hearty breakfast she'd wanted in Gargrave. They talked a little, about the good weather and the need to water the plants and whether they might sit out later, but both women had a preoccupied look. The killer was still out there, even on such a perfect summer's day.

'Shall you be going back north, Frank? Colette told me how busy you are.'

'I thought I might stay till tomorrow, if that won't be any trouble.'

'Oh do. It's been so nice having you here.'

Colette suddenly shook herself, then smiled. Her eyes seemed to hint at further lovemaking in Crane's three-quarter bed. Her spirits looked to be rising with the clear light, her determination to live freely and enjoy life taking hold again.

He sipped the fresh coffee. It was very good. He'd made instant earlier, but Dora had percolated some Columbian. He forced a cheerful smile, tried to decide how to get the ball rolling about going to the shopping centre.

But Colette solved the problem. 'Oh, let's go to town. I'm longing to look at the shops again. And there's quite a lot going on in the square today. Charity events: choir singing and a brass band and so forth.'

Dora looked anxious. 'Would it be safe, Frank, do you think?'

'I . . . think so, there'll be so many people about. And there are always a couple of police keeping tabs on you.'

'Dora darling, I feel we've got to make a start at living as normally as possible. And we've got Frank with us as well as the bobbies.'

'Won't it be boring for you, Frank?'

'Sounds like fun. And if anyone deserves to get out and about it's you two.'

'That's jolly nice of you.' Dora touched his hand. 'I'm sure you'd much rather have a drive to the coast and a pub lunch.'

Dora had it dead right.

★   ★   ★

Gordy keyed the pad nervously.

'Yes.'

'They've left the house, Lenny, Crane and the women.'

'On foot?'

'That's right.'

'Heading towards the centre?'

'Correct.'

'And they're in place: Chas, Jason, Mick?'

'They've all rung in.'

'Jason's not wearing that striped fucking *blazer* this time, I hope.'

'T-shirts, denims, trainers, that class of gear. All three.'

' 'Cause they'd better blend in with every other fucker or there'll be trouble. Big time.'

'They know that, Lenny.'

'They'd better . . . '

Gordy cleared his phone with a hand that shook slightly.

'Christ, what's the mad sod going to *do*?' Wayne said.

'Does anyone *ever* know what he's going to do till he does it?' Gordy said, sighing. 'Anyway, the stupid bitch'll be out of it today, that's for sure, and we'll be out of here for good. Am I sick of the sight of Eastern fucking Lane.'

'Too right. Sod this for a game of soldiers.'

It wasn't far to the centre and they went on foot. He told them they knew the police were always around, but to act as naturally as possible. They all looked very normal as they strolled along, making a good pretence of casual chat. But he could sense a wariness and tension in them that he knew would always be there whenever they stepped out of the house.

He'd given a single cursory glance along the road as he'd walked down the drive of Dora's semi, but windscreens had glinted in sunlight and he couldn't tell if any of the parked cars were occupied.

They moved on steadily, through the station underpass and along the diagonal alley-way, with its cafés and hairdressers and estate agents, and then across a street of shops that lay just above the complex called Wolsey Place, whose broad mall led to the central square.

Colette began to enjoy herself, nerves gradually forgotten. She wanted to stop everywhere, to wander into boutiques and hold garments against her body, to gaze at glittering displays of bracelets, watches and rings, to linger outside shoe shops and shops that sold travel goods.

'I'll need a new case, Dora, for when we have that first weekend away,' she said firmly. 'Something with a posh name to impress the flunkeys.'

Crane watched their backs. Old men shuffled about, young T-shirted men swaggered, men with wives and children looked bored and harassed. Any one of them, or none, could be Brewer. They finally walked down a ramp into the square itself. Crane placed the buildings in which Tetley had said he'd plant people, scrutinizing the square with powerful lenses: the bank, the church, the library and The Peacocks. He checked his watch. Eleven-fifteen. The square looked to be as busy as it was going to get. The charity day was for the purchase of hospital equipment. To their right, school-children stood on a temporary structure and were conducted in their choir singing by an enthusiastic young master in a white shirt and denims. The sweet, artless voices carried in the clear air, cutting through the talk and laughter of the bustling crowd. Near the library a small compound had been laid out around which little boys and girls drove small motorized dodgems. Bandsmen were gathering with their gleaming instruments in front of the tall, ornamental iron gates that were only opened for access. At the other side of the square men were calling prices at market stalls piled with vegetables, flowers and fruit. Clowns juggled in front of them or walked on stilts, and a woman held big gas-filled balloons that bobbed and glittered in the sun.

'I need a watch-strap or a bracelet,' Colette said. 'This one's almost worn out and I'd hate to lose the watch. Tony bought it for me. I have an idea there's a man in the craft market who does watches and straps.'

'That's right,' Dora said. 'Along at the far end.'

They walked towards the fruit stalls, clustered at the opening of a cavernous passage that held the rest of the market stalls. It looked to run between the outer walls of the two shopping blocks, which had been connected by a high roof. Crane followed uneasily. He knew that Tetley would be counting on him to keep them out in the open as long as possible. Too much could happen in the covered areas, where the crowds might be even denser, too quickly for the police to react in time.

Though he was becoming tenser, the women were now beginning to relax. Maybe it was the lighthearted Saturday atmosphere and their first real chance to go on a shopping spree. The cheerful crowd seemed to present no kind of threat.

But Brewer was about. Crane knew Tetley had it right. He could be a few yards from them right now. They made their way towards a stall at the far end of the cavern, where a man with an eye-piece magnifier studied the insides of a watch for a woman who stood before him.

What if Brewer had dressed himself as a woman? Had Tetley taken that on board? Brewer might believe he could get closer to Colette without causing as much suspicion. A little old lady who quietly did the business from behind her shopping bag, then lost herself in the crowd. In the end, Crane found himself watching women more carefully than men, especially if they walked alone and had a stick or a stoop, or had hair that looked a little too well tended. But then it struck him that maybe a *policewoman* had disguised herself as a pensioner to keep near his group. It was a nightmare.

They came to the stall where the watchmender sat. He had given the woman he was serving a repair ticket, and now began to lay out watch-straps and bracelets for Colette to look at. He worried Crane too. He was greyish and sixtyish and talked in a quiet courteous voice. He wore an old silver-grey jacket that looked to be mohair. It seemed to go with men who knew their way around watches on market stalls. Crane couldn't get it off his mind about Brewer being a courteous old man in Gargrave. The mohair jacket might be one of his inspired touches. He didn't stop to think how Brewer could possibly have positioned himself behind this stall. He knew he was getting paranoid.

And then it happened. A gun blast. His heart lurched as the explosion echoed along the passage. He thrust his arms round the women as people started or gave little screams of alarm. But the watchmender had scarcely reacted, to what had to be the boom of a shot-gun.

'A balloon,' he said, with a shrug. 'They sometimes over-inflate one. It carries along here with the high ceiling. I think the strap or the bracelet would look equally nice, miss.'

'I'll . . . take the bracelet,' Colette said, face pale, lips quivering.

'I can attach it, if you wish.'

She nodded and he rapidly fitted the bracelet, took Colette's note and made change from a little wooden tray, indented for different coin sizes. 'Thank you, miss. Do pay me a visit if you ever decide to buy a new watch. Mine are about half what you'd pay in the shops. I don't carry the overheads, you see.'

His warm smile slowly passed to another customer, and they returned to the square, its light almost blinding at the end of the shady cavern. The women were still shaken and subdued. The bursting balloon sounding like a gunshot had flipped their minds back on to Lenny Brewer too. They came out on to the stilted clowns and the jugglers and the hoarse-voiced men who shouted prices. Crane felt a wave of fatigue. It was the intense strain of watching over them. He had to tell himself he was supposed to be top dressing here, that the entire square was watched over by plainclothes policemen and women, all watching every move they made. But it gave him no comfort.

'I'd like to get Marks out of the way, if no one minds,' Dora said. 'Ciabatta bread and salad and something nice for dinner. Your choice, Frank, what shall it be: Italian, Chinese, Indian? Or straightforward English, of course.'

'I'm fine with anything, Dora.' He tried to sound polite through his preoccupation. It meant going inside again. Dora was already edging towards the entrance of The Peacocks complex. He felt he had to keep them in the open for at least another fifteen minutes. Just

276

then the choir burst into song again with 'The Ash Grove'.

'Would you mind if we listened to the kids for a little while? I once sang in a school choir myself.' He forced a smile. 'Would you believe?'

'But we'd *love* to,' Dora said. 'It's your day out as much as ours.'

Some day out. He'd just about got his nerves under control again. And then he suddenly caught sight of Luke Tetley. He stood near the flower-sellers, as if trying to decide what to buy. He wore a lightweight jerkin, chinos, and an open-neck shirt. The sun gleamed on his mop of fair hair. He watched Crane impassively for several seconds, then gave the smallest narrowing of the eyelids of one eye. Crane responded with the ghost of a nod. He felt slightly relieved. The gang's all here, Tetley's wink seemed to say.

They came to the group of people gathered around the singing children, neat and clean in their white tops. Even here, Crane was agitated. What if Brewer struck now, among the mums and dads? He could see the reaction. The cries of the women, the screams and tears of the children, Brewer legging it along Wolsey Place, surrounded by people of his own. People who'd look as anonymous as Tetley's task force.

He tried not to take his eyes off Colette. But Brewer would know how to distract him, by one of his goons. And then Brewer would only need two bullets, one at a pinch, or one thrust of a blade, to inflict mortal damage.

But Tetley was around. And Crane trusted him. He was certain he'd be as much in control as it was possible to be. He'd have some of his people here right now, dotted among the audience. Crane could relax. He'd done his bit by getting Colette to the shopping centre. But he couldn't relax. He felt as if concentrated acid was punching holes in the lining of his stomach.

The song ended, to lengthy applause. It was to be the last before the lunch break. The choir-master turned to thank them and to ask them to be generous when the collectors came round, who now rattled their tins. The money would go towards a much-needed scanner.

Crane and the women made their donations, children were collected by proud parents, the little crowd began to break up, to merge with the general crowd. Crane tried to spot Tetley again, but couldn't. He wondered if they'd seen anyone, anyone at all, who could be Brewer. Maybe those powerful binocs had picked up on a suspicious pattern of behaviour not easily detected at ground level. Crane hoped to Christ they had and passed it to the ones on the ground through the ear-pieces. But what if it was one of Brewer's people deliberately acting in a suspicious way to divert attention from Brewer himself? Surely Tetley would have taken that into account.

He felt slightly queasy with the heat and a tension it was beyond him to control. But the women seemed to be relaxing now. They'd had a shock but it had simply been a balloon bursting. Colette was beginning to revel in her new-found freedom again, was forcing herself to put the fear on hold. She chatted to Dora with that cheerful, dogged animation that the other always reacted to. It was how she'd found the courage to have Colette live with her in the first place.

Time was running in long-play mode. It had been barely half an hour since they'd walked into the square. It seemed like two. Crane began to fret now because Brewer *hadn't* made his move. Why not? They'd spent plenty of time in the open. Easy targets. Maybe Brewer had had a change of plan. Maybe Tetley had been fed duff info. What if Brewer, cunning as ever, had deliberately arranged to leak information that Colette had to be seen off at the weekend, to muddy the waters and distract the police? While his real aim was to pick her off later. Catch them on the back foot. Had *that* occured to Tetley?

Other music was making its impression: hurdy gurdy style for the dodgem circuit, honky tonk from where the clowns and jugglers strutted about. The bandsmen had taken over from the choir and could be heard tuning their instruments. Guilt was added to Crane's tension to see a Colette who'd never looked better. Her arms were bare and slightly freckled in the floral dress, and her hair, falling to her shoulders, was glossy in the summer light. Her eyes seemed to gleam with the sheer delight of being among ordinary people. She was OD-ing on freedom, after the long, sad, dreary months on Blackbird.

'I really must go to Marks now,' Dora said apologetically. 'They tend to run out of certain things on a busy day. Perhaps we could have lunch in the atrium café . . . '

They were walking across the square for a third time, in the direction of The Peacocks. If it was to be M & S and then lunch, they'd be off the square for at least an hour. He'd thought earlier it would be more dangerous to walk in the covered areas, forgetting that these days malls and stores were stuffed with CCTV cameras and security guards. Brewer could do without that kind of attention, even if he was aiming to do a spectacular.

But Crane was beginning to feel certain Brewer had called it off. He must have recognized a face in the crowd, maybe even Tetley's. They said the Brewers could *smell* police.

He had mixed reactions about that too. He'd been geared up to Brewer making his move today. Whatever happened, at least it would be over. And if the luck had run with Tetley he'd have been able to drive back north with a weight off his mind. But if Brewer had sensed a set-up, the danger for Colette just went on.

But then it happened, at incredible speed. He pelted towards Crane on a rear diagonal to his left. He heard the tense words, 'Stay clear, Frank, I'll keep her covered.'

It was Tetley. He tore past, pushing Dora aside with a shoulder and grabbing Colette, to huddle her against himself. Both women were too stunned to make a sound. The second he had her clasped against his hunched body another man scurried out of the crowd. Crane glimpsed a beige linen cap and sunglasses. Then he saw the flash of a knife-blade. It plunged into Tetley's back with incredible speed and force, again and again.

Crane leapt forward and seized the man, wrapping his arms round his chest and holding his arms pinioned. But even before he could do that he'd thrust in the knife again, for one last time.

15

He was like a man demented, kicking and writing in Crane's arms. Crane struck the hand that held the knife with the edge of his own and all his force, heard the knife skitter along the ground. Where were the *police*?

There'd been several seconds of appalled silence and then it was pandemonium. People gasped and shrieked as Tetley sank slowly to the ground, half-dragging Colette, chalk-white with shock, but who shook herself free and managed to keep her balance. Some people ran off, not wanting to know, some stood open-mouthed and motionless, some backed away to what they seemed to think was a safe distance, then also gawped. The sunglasses had fallen from the man Crane held, who'd stopped struggling now, accepting he couldn't free himself. The linen cap was askew, on curly hair. And Crane knew the face, knew it very well, and it wasn't Brewer in disguise. It was the face of Robert Marshall.

'Christ!' Crane broke out. 'Christ almighty! You insane sod, do you know what you've *done*? You've knifed a *policeman*! He's *police*! He wasn't attacking her, he was *protecting* her. He had her covered. You've blown the whole *thing*!'

He stared at Crane wildly, over his shoulder, eyelids flickering. 'I've been *watching* him!' he cried. 'I've been watching the bastard ever since you *came* here. Wherever you all went he went *too*. He has a gun. I saw it when he grabbed hold of her. It was so small you could hardly see it, but I saw it.'

'Of *course* he had a fucking gun! He'd have been issued with one when he was trying to trap a man like Brewer. Oh *God*!'

The music had been cut off now, the dodgems halted, the stall-holders no longer shouted. A silence had filtered over the square like the one in Whitehall on Remembrance Day. Two well-built men, casually dressed, now pushed their way through the crowd, calling, 'Police, make way . . .'

They looked from Crane to Marshall to the man lying on the ground unconscious, blood now trickling from beneath him in a thin stream. One of them fell to his knees, began to test pulses. The other looked back at Crane. 'We know you're Frank Crane,' he said, 'and we know all about the women. But who are these two and what's happened?'

'I need to see your warrant cards,' Crane said curtly.

The standing man looked annoyed and swore under his breath, but took it out. It looked to be in order. He was called Raynor and he was a DC.

'Both of them.'

'For fuck's *sake!*' the kneeling man muttered, but also took it out. That looked to be genuine too. 'Look, Crane,' he said, 'I need to get an ambulance if this guy's going to have a chance.' He produced a police radio.

'Why don't you recognize your own colleague?' Crane demanded. 'DS Tetley. You must be from the local force.'

Both men watched him in a stunned silence, mouths falling open. Everyone was very still, the wide-eyed crowd, the police detectives, the two trembling women, Dora with both hands to her face, as if to ward off blows.

'He's no one *we* know,' the kneeling man said. 'Never seen him before. You, Gerry?'

The other shook his head.

'Has he got a gun?' Crane said.

The kneeling man carefully lifted an arm by the sleeve of the jerkin. A small, snub-nosed automatic lay shining bluely in the noon glare. At its side lay a false nose, the type of prosthetic that was now so well made as to be barely distinguishable from the real thing. And yesterday evening Crane had seen

Tetley mainly in a poor light.

'That's got to be a wig,' he said, controlling his voice with difficulty.

The other gave the man's hair a slight tug. The wig was very tightly fitted but it moved. It revealed a band of close-cut brown hair.

'There'll be facial pads,' he muttered. 'Contact lenses to give him blue eyes. Maybe something covering his own teeth. And the shoes, they'll have platforms.'

The kneeling man carefully drew back a leg of the chinos. The shoes had the build-up that had given Tetley height.

'Look at his right arm, just above the wrist,' he said in the same low voice, remembering what Adam at Jarvis Motors had seen. 'There'll be a tattoo of a bird.'

There was. It looked to be the likeness of a hawk or an eagle.

'It can't be . . . Lenny *Brewer*!' Raynor said. There was a near reverent tone in his hushed voice.

'You must have seen photos of him . . . '

'The last we've got was taken during his granny's funeral with a long focus. It's got to be the only time in the last few years he's looked like himself.'

'Well, you'll be able to check him out when you get him to the station. Or the morgue. But it's definitely Brewer,' Crane said. 'Look, didn't you see him come to Mrs Powell's last night? He was pretending to be a copper then.'

Raynor stared at him, still trying to make sense of it all. The kneeling man was speaking urgently into his radio. 'We weren't on duty last night, it was a different team. Did he *act* suspiciously? We've been treading a fine line, you know. If we'd stopped everyone who came to the house the women would accuse us of being heavy-handed.'

Crane nodded. He remembered that Tetley/Brewer had been hunched over when he'd shown him the forged warrant card, which would have made it difficult for anyone in Eastern Lane to see what he was doing. And Crane *had* actually let him in the house, gone out and sat with him in his car. It must have seemed completely bona. He'd certainly had Crane fooled. A *second* time.

'Well,' he said, 'Brewer pretending to be a DS talked me into arranging to have Colette and Mrs Powell in this square this morning.'

Both women gasped.

'All right,' Raynor said, 'save it all for later. Who are *you* then?'

'Marshall,' the other said, in a low voice. 'Robert Marshall. And if I'd not got to the murdering bastard in time she'd be *dead*. A lot of fucking good you all were.'

'Were you the only police shadowing us?' Crane broke in. The full impact of the danger she'd been in suddenly hit him like a kick in the guts.

'How many did you *expect?*' Raynor said irritably. 'We've had people on obbo round the clock at Mrs Powell's place ever since Colette got back to Woking. Combat trained,' he added flatly, 'to deal with Brewer whether he'd been in the Paras or not.'

'But when we came here, to a crowded square, surely you'd have sent for back-up?'

'It was considered *low risk*, Crane. Daylight, Saturday, middle of town. Brewer just doesn't work that way. He likes to see them off at night, in multi-storeys, pub car-parks.'

'He worked that way this time, right,' Crane said harshly. 'It seems to me, the way he operated was to get people thinking he did things one particular way and then to do the opposite.'

They heard the distant sound of an ambulance then and the sirens of the blues and twos. 'Robert Marshall,' Raynor said to him, 'these are your rights . . .'

Marshall seemed neither to hear or care. He was gazing at Colette in the old compulsive way, the man he'd stabbed with such ferocity ignored. The steady trickle of blood from beneath Brewer had made a little pool. He had to be dead. Well, Marshall had sworn he'd look after Colette, make absolutely sure no harm ever came to her. He couldn't have done a better job. He must have been around Crane and the women all the time, also disguised, in the shades and the linen cap. That was how he'd seen Brewer hovering round them too. The man Crane had taken for a genuine policeman had simply been a predator to Marshall. Someone he'd decided could only be Brewer. And thank Christ too, Crane thought, guts still churning with the danger she'd been in.

'Marshall is Colette's stepfather,' he told Raynor. 'It's another long story that led to this.'

'He'll have plenty of time to tell it at the station,' Raynor muttered. He was gazing with a kind of awe at the bleeding figure. It was beginning to strike him too, the scale of what had happened. *The* Lenny Brewer, one of the hardest men in organized crime, tied to at least half-a-dozen killings they knew were down to him but couldn't be proved. Crane knew how his mind was working. There were brownie points to be had here, just by being in the right place at the right time.

'Go easy on the bloke, will you,' Crane said softly. 'He's done you all a favour. Just make sure he gets an intelligent brief and try not to make it any worse for him than it already is. He's right. If he'd not been here with the knife she'd be dead. He knows it, I know it and you know it.'

The detective looked back at Marshall, who still gazed at the shocked and silent Colette. He seemed oblivious to the trouble he was in. 'He was armed, Frank, with intent,' Raynor said, voice equally almost a whisper. 'You can't do the vigilante stuff without serious comebacks. But I hear what you're saying. I'll put my people in the picture. You ask me, if we were right in the fucking head we'd give the poor bugger a medal, taking out a piece of shit like Brewer.'

Paramedics came running from the ambulance, which had nosed slowly into the square, still packed with onlookers. They were followed by SOC people, who'd need to gather careful forensic evidence, even though a dozen people had seen Marshall stab Brewer. Uniformed police began urging the crowd to disperse and were preparing to tape up the area of the body, which had been rapidly confirmed to be as dead as it looked.

Crane and the two women were briefly ignored, but he knew they'd be in for a long haul of questions and statements before they could get away.

'What happens now, Frank?' Colette said, her lips still quivering and the skin of her arms in gooseflesh, even in this heat. 'I mean now he's dead.'

Crane's spirits hit minus zero. He'd not had time to think this far. But what happened now was that she was in as much trouble as she'd ever been. Not only was the contract still in place but Donny had now lost his only son because of That Woman. Vengeance would be swift and certain, unless Colette was hidden in the deepest hole the police could dig.

★ ★ ★

Crane drove back north in a low state of mind. The women were now being guarded more carefully than ever before. The police had reached exactly the same conclusion as Crane, that Donny would want instant retribution the minute he had the news of Lenny.

They'd spent a long time at the station helping the police unwind the bizarre sequence of events that had led to the stabbing. Dora and Colette had explained in their own halting words what had happened in the square and signed statements to that effect. They'd then been taken off by a matronly-looking policewoman. Crane was asked to stay behind with Raynor and a DCI, as it soon became obvious they'd be talking about things they didn't, at this stage, want the women to hear.

'What do you think Brewer's game was, Frank?' the DCI asked, when the door closed.

'We'll never know for certain, but my feeling is that when he was hunched over her he was going to kill her then. Two shots to the heart, he had the skills. We'd scarcely have heard a sound with all the noise in the square. Then I reckon he was going to rush off as if someone *else* had shot her and he was in pursuit. He'd be sure I'd not go after him because to me he was police and knew what he was doing. All my attention would be on Colette and I'd be expecting a bunch of police detectives to come tearing up. Apart from which, he'd told me that whatever happened I'd not to get involved in the action as I'd only get in the way of trained people.'

The DCI was a thick-set man with broken veins in a reddish face and dark hair turning to grey. He looked like he'd been born with an expression of weary scepticism. 'You really think Brewer would take a chance like *that*? He's never done *anything* high profile before. We only wish he had.'

'I think he wanted to show me how clever

he was. We'd given him a run around up north, Colette and me, and I don't think he liked it. Trouble is, I reckon he'd have got away with it if Marshall hadn't been around. By the time he'd got to the other end of The Peacocks he'd be looking like a different bloke altogether. He could do the voices and the make-up and he was the sharpest bad lot I've ever known.'

The two police didn't like that and it showed. But Crane knew they knew he was right. 'She'll *have* to go back in the programme, Frank,' the DCI said heavily. 'You know what's going to happen, Donny'll go berserk. He's never been renowned for his self-control. He'll get her seen to if it costs him fifty grand. She must see the danger she's putting herself in. And us.'

Crane shook his head. 'She'll never go back. I know you must think she's certifiable, but she knows the risks and she's ready to take them.'

'You've *got* to talk her into it. I don't want any of my people injured because she's not wired right. We've not forgotten what happened to the two young chaps who were guarding her in Bradford. You're her boy-friend, you're the only one with real clout. Can you stay on here?'

'Sorry, I'm a one-man band. I've got to go

back north. If I don't work I don't eat.'

'Come back next weekend then. Will you do that for us? In the meantime I'll be putting the pressure on myself.'

He had to make the promise, knowing it was a total waste of time. The three of them were finally driven to Dora's place, where the women spent the rest of the day in a daze, unable to concentrate. In the end Crane put together a scratch meal himself. He needn't have bothered, as none of them ate much. Nothing was said about it, but Crane knew they'd worked it out for themselves that Lenny's death wasn't an end to it, just a brief pause. And maybe not brief.

All preoccupied with their own thoughts they sat in front of a flickering television that went unheeded. Dora went off to bed about ten. Crane guessed she was anxious to take the sleeping pill that would give her temporary peace of mind. When she'd gone, Colette suddenly began to speak, as if she knew only too well what Crane was thinking. 'I'm not going back in the programme, whatever you say. My father had a long illness and a lot of pain, and we all knew he was going to die at the end of it. Well, that's how I'd be if I went back in the programme. It would be Blackbird Common all over again, fretting and being scared and lonely all the time, and eating too much. And knowing that they'd get me in the end anyway. If I'm going to die I want to be here with Dora.'

Later, she crept into Crane's room. She didn't want sex. Not tonight. She just wanted to be held.

★ ★ ★

Crane went back to the normal routines of normal life. He went to see a woman whose teenage daughter had run away from home. She'd not got on with her stepfather. The woman had hinted at things she found difficult to talk about openly. Crane could have told her how often stepfathers were the cause of girls taking off. The truth was that stepfathers so often saw in stepdaughters something that had drawn them to their mothers in the first place. Except that this was a fresh, young, firm-breasted version that seemed to be a monumental turn-on for the creeps. Take Marshall and Colette.

He took the case, and alerted Nick Gardner first as usual, his London contact, as girls legging it nearly always seemed to run one way and to the worst possible destination.

As soon as he spoke, Gardner said, 'Well, you did have fun in Woking, didn't you?'

'Don't remind me. It's not over yet by a long chalk. Me and the Woking police are convinced she's in more danger than ever. Whoever gets the contract won't fuck about like Lenny did, that's for sure.'

There was a silence, then Gardner said, 'You've not *heard* about Donny then?'

'What about Donny?' he said uneasily.

'He's had a stroke. Major. When they slipped him the news about Lenny. I reckon he was always a blood-pressure freak with that temper of his. He's in intensive care, but they reckon if he comes round he'll be half the man he was. The press'll be on to it any time now.'

'That's a hell of a turn-up . . . . . . '

'They were giving your friend Colette seven days top whack. They reckon he'd have hired the best gun in London, if not New York, name your price. But he's out of it now. And what's left, if he makes it from the ICU, won't be worth bothering about. There could be so much brain damage he might not even remember Lenny's actually bought it.'

'As bad as that.'

'Inside minutes of a flat-line.'

Crane thought about this. 'Donny's other people: won't *they* want to see the contract through?'

'No chance. What you need to remember,

Frank, is that Donny's people are mainly middle-aged, just like Donny. They've about had enough of the hassle that goes with drugs and toms and illegals. It was a joint decision to tidy up the money and phase into legal operations. They wanted to relax and put their feet up. Apart from that they didn't *like* Lenny. He was a father's son and he'd been a Para, two reasons for thinking he was God almighty. You ask me, I think they broke out the Krug the day Marshall put the knife in. And with him gone they'll get a bigger share of what loot's going. They always felt he got too much for doing fuck-all anyway. And they're old-style villains, yes. They could go along with someone being rubbed out who was causing them serious aggravation, but that sort of sadistic stuff Lenny got off on, well, believe it or not, they thought it was common.'

Crane said, 'But Donny's family . . . there's a wife and daughter, right?'

'Always kept their heads down, like nice old-style villains' families. They knew what Donny did and that was it. They genuinely knew sod-all about the nuts and bolts. It was a kind of insurance against when the police came round trying to feel Donny's collar. They knew there was a contract out on Colette, everyone did, and they'd have a good

297

idea who'd be pulling the trigger. They'll be sobbing their eyes out about Lenny gone and Donny as good as, but they'll not want to carry anything on . . . '

Gardner had it right. The papers were soon to report that Donny Brewer was a fragile shell of the powerful underworld figure he'd once been, his brain and memory acutely impaired. His wife and daughter were warned not to remind him that Lenny was dead as the shock would certainly kill him. Lenny was back in Africa, freelancing, if Donny could find enough operating brain cells to ask.

* * *

It was Sunday morning. Crane's door-bell rang. He opened the door on a Terry Jones who gave him one of his rare smiles.

'Terry! Come in.'

'You're not rushing off?'

'Nothing that won't wait. Go through.'

'No, the kitchen'll do fine. I'll perch here if that's all right.'

They both sat on stools at the breakfast-bar and Crane poured coffee.

'They're very pleased in Leeds, Frank. Their DCI rang me Friday. He'd had a bad time, two of his best DCs getting done over, Colette doing a moonlight. But knowing that

298

twisted sod is out of it, well, you're the blue-eyed boy. You did as they asked, you went back down there. But to come up with a result like *that*. Believe me, without you he knows they'd still be searching for the swine five years out. He didn't *say* that, you know what cagey buggers the police are, but the inference was there.'

Crane smiled wryly. 'The only thing is, I blew it, Terry. He had me totally foxed. And not for the first time.'

'What does it matter? He's gone. That murdering father of his has gone too, or as good as. And I'm told the rest of their people legged it overnight. They'd all decided Woking was not a good place to be. All right, they were all getting ready to settle for the cocoa and cardigans, but Lenny wasn't. He was youngish, no older than you, and he'd not have settled for collecting rent money. He'd have started up a new outfit with other hand-picked hard cases . . . '

But Crane still looked on sourly. He sipped some of the coffee. 'Terry it was pure chance. It was Marshall who saw him off. She'd almost certainly have bought it without him.'

'I know that, but it was you getting the show off the ground.'

'Let's be honest. She should never have sent me to Woking in the first place. She was in the programme and if she'd stayed in it and not involved me she'd have been safe. As it was she nearly got herself killed.'

'Life's full of those sorts of chances, Frank.'

Jones shook his head in resignation. It had been exactly the same when Crane had first made it from uniform to plain clothes. He'd begun to work long hours, had carefully thought things through and was the sharpest knife in the box. But now and then even Crane had got it wrong. And Jones would bawl him out, as DI's did. But Crane hadn't been defensive then either. Crane swallowed blame whole, would begin to mull over how he could have got it wrong, would brood endlessly. In the end it would be Jones himself cutting him the slack, playing it down, telling him not to take it so *hard*, chill out, for Christ's sake, here, have a drink.

And Crane was still taking it hard, was still wearing self-reproach like a hair-shirt. All right, he'd got it wrong about 'Luke Tetley', but in Brewer, it seemed to Jones, Crane had been up against a mind as keen as his own, however depraved. 'Frank, you've got to accept that none of it could have happened as it did without your input. Colette would probably never have got her old confidence back. You were exactly what she needed, a big strong bloke taking an interest in her. You

300

were the catalyst, giving her the courage to do what she did, break with the programme, go back to Woking. And you got her back there in one piece, right, despite a bugged car. She'd have been no safer *in* the programme, not with Lenny. He'd have got there sooner or later. Either way she'd have been a goner. You know that's the truth. She'd never have been safe.'

Crane shrugged, sighed. 'I just thank God the kid's alive and out of it.'

'Well, look, son, whatever *you* think, the Leeds people just love the bottom line. They feel vindicated for the kicking their men got. And my friend is keen to make sure you're looked after. He's a high-flyer, a mason, and he knows some very big people. And big people have special problems because of all that money they're sitting on. They tend to ask my friend if he can put them in touch with a really first-class private man when they need to make sure their daughter's boyfriend isn't wanting to marry her just for the loot, that type of thing. He'd like to throw some of those enquiries your way. And let's face it, Leeds is first division country.'

Crane's mood began to lighten at long last. Leeds was only seven or eight miles away, centre to centre, but it could have been a hundred for all the work that ever came his

301

way from there. 'Well, that *is* good news, Terry. Thanks a lot.'

'He'll not forget. He's not a man who forgets anything.' He glanced at his watch. 'Well, must go. I've promised to take Jenny to the coast. Do I need it, the week I've had.'

'Give Jenny my regards,' Crane said, walking the other to the door. Out on the step, Jones turned. 'It worked out *right*, Frank, that's all that matters now. Things always did have a habit of working out right around you. You always used to make me think what Napoleon always asked about young officers being put forward for promotion, 'Does he have luck?''

As they shook hand he added quietly, 'Christ, Frank, I wish you were back.'

★ ★ ★

Marshall was eventually brought to trial, with Crane, Colette and Dora called as witnesses. He'd been fixed up with a brilliant defence counsel, who'd quietly discarded Marshall's unhealthy sexual obsession with Colette. He presented his concern for her safety as a stepfather who'd come to love and cherish her as if she were his own flesh and blood. He'd known, as the entire country did, that someone was intending to kill her, that a so-called contract had been taken out on her, and he'd been driven to any lengths to protect her, while accepting the seriousness of having armed himself. At one stage, Crane caught Colette's eye, who gave him a small wry smile, but other eyes in the packed courtroom were suspiciously moist.

The judge had handed down the shortest sentence he must have felt he could impose under the circumstances. He pointed out that though Marshall had convinced himself he was protecting his stepdaughter from a man determined to kill her, he didn't know that for certain. He might well have killed the police officer that Mr Crane had been convinced he was. Quite apart from which, members of the public must never imagine they could take the law into their own hands, whatever sort of right they supposed themselves to have.

He gave Marshall five years, which with good behaviour would mean just over two. But the *Daily Mail* had led the tabloids in whipping up righteous indignation about even a sentence as nominal as that. How could society, they demanded, imprison a man who'd rid society of murdering scum like Lenny Brewer, son of a murdering father? It demanded his sentence be suspended and that he be freed instantly. It set rolling a

FREE ROBERT MARSHALL campaign. 'Yes' coupons arrived by the sackload.

★ ★ ★

Crane's mobile rang. 'Frank Crane.'

'Hello, Frank Crane, fancy buying an old friend a drink?'

'That can't be . . . Colette?'

'I'm in the Glass-house.'

'What are you doing there?'

'Where are *you*?'

'Between car and office. Give me fifteen minutes to see to my mail. But what are you *doing* there?'

'Can't *wait* to see you.' She broke the connection.

When he walked in the big lounge, with its glittering chandeliers and its many mirrors, she was sitting at a glass table in one of the cubicles with the frosted-glass partitions. 'Hello, Frank,' she said, in that husky voice he'd got to know so well.

'Colette!' He grasped her arms, kissed her cheek. 'I never thought I'd ever see you back here.'

'It's so good to see you, Frank.'

'But what are you *doing* here?' He sat down opposite her.

'I was taking a couple of days' leave, so I

thought how nice it would be to look up an old friend.'

He smiled. 'About which your old friend thinks you're being economical with the truth.'

She also smiled. 'I never could get much past you.'

A bar-girl put down a little dish of salted nuts and asked what she could get them. 'Two G and Ts, ice and lemon,' Crane told her, not needing to check.

When she'd gone, Colette said, 'My old boss at the financial advisers, he kept my mobile number. He rang last week, saying there was a good vacancy. He hinted it could lead to a junior partnership.'

Crane looked puzzled. 'And you told him in his dreams . . . '

She watched him for a few seconds in silence. 'I almost did. And then I got to thinking. It was a job I was good at . . . I liked the people — '

She broke off as the bar-girl put down their drinks and took Crane's money. She picked up her glass with a sigh of pleasure, trickled in tonic. 'Do I need this after two hundred and fifty miles on the motorway.'

She was wearing a short collarless, woollen jacket in oatmeal and a black turtle-neck in what looked to be silk, above a pleated skirt in checks of muted blue. It came somewhere between formal and informal and would be just right for an interview with a man who already knew how competent she looked in the long-line jackets and the well-cut trousers. The chestnut colouring had now grown out of her almost Nordic blonde hair, which had been taken back into what Crane believed was a french pleat. He said, 'You *can't* want to come back here. After Blackbird Common, the dreadful time you had.'

She shrugged, sipped some of her drink. He guessed she was now back to her original willowy shape. She watched him pensively and he remembered what a lot that very slight cast in one of her amber eyes did for her. 'You know, I was beginning to get nostalgic. Not for Bradford, but for Yorkshire. I couldn't get it out of my mind, the drive we took to Gargrave, and then on to Ilkley. It was like being on acid, the way I saw the moors and the fells and the river. If I did come back I'd not live here, it would be twenty miles out in one of the villages or little towns.'

'You'd earn twice as much in Surrey.'

'Maybe there's more to it than the size of the pay-cheques.'

'I thought you wanted to stay with Dora. After all you'd been through together.'

Her unfocused gaze passed his face, to

where the central tables were beginning to fill with people from the nearby offices. 'We thought we'd be together for a year at least. They were good days too. Just to be *free*. Not to be watched any more by anyone. Not to jump out of our chairs when the door-bell rang. We got jobs, began to see old friends, go to pubs, restaurants, the cinema . . .

'But in the end . . . ' She glanced back at him. 'In the end I think we both began to realize we needed to take a fresh look at things. We didn't say as much, but I think we both knew we'd not really be able to move on if we didn't live our own lives. Apart from that, Dora's husband rang not long ago asking if he could take her for a meal.'

'He wants to come back?'

'He's asked her if she'll think about it. He's had time to do a lot of thinking too. He knows she needed his support, knows he was weak about clearing off. But there's no other woman involved and he misses her terribly. She was bitter, very bitter, but I know she wants him back. They've been together half a lifetime and it was a happy marriage until . . . '

'I'm sure he suffered as much as Dora in his own way.'

'That's what I said. And at least the Brewers *paid* for what they did to Tony.

307

Things will never be the same for any of us, but they've a chance now to make a new start, if she's prepared to forgive and forget. She's certainly not interested in anyone else.'

'How about you? Have you . . . found anyone else?'

Her mobile face slowly lost expression. 'Oh, I've been out now and then with some bloke or other. Dora was *keen* for me to. Decent types who had good careers.' She sighed. 'It didn't work. I was my own problem. I found it near impossible to be around normal blokes any more. Couldn't relate, just couldn't relate. They'd had the life most men have: the job, the match, the pub, the clubs, a fortnight in the Algarve. They saw me exactly as I used to look, but . . . but I was reacting as the woman I am now. And they couldn't really begin to make much sense of the woman I am now. I couldn't expect them to. We were like people who spoke different languages. Does . . . does that begin to make any sense?'

'To me, yes.'

It took Crane back to his early police days, when it had become difficult to mix with old friends, who'd not seen the things he'd seen and never would, the bloodstained human debris that society needed him to help clear up, but wanted to be spared the details.

They sat in silence for a time. Crane was surprised how much he'd missed her. He didn't do missing people, not after Vicky. He looked at the confident woman she'd now become, with her toned body and her blonde looks. Maybe he had had a little to do with helping to change her from the lonely, apathetic creature he'd first known. He said, 'If Harry and Dora do get back together I suppose you'll need to look for a place of your own.'

'It would make sense anyway. I've got some spare money. No one knows better than me it needs to be a down-payment on a place of my own before prices rise any further.'

'But in a Yorkshire village? You can't be serious.'

'I really have given it a lot of thought.'

'I daresay you'll find the blokes up here speak in tongues too.'

She began to smile. 'Perhaps not all.'

'Another drink?'

'A meal would be nice. I once gave you dinner at that dump on Blackbird. You said you'd have me back to eat at your place, but you never did.'

'By then you were halfway across West Yorkshire in a blonde wig.'

'Can I have it now then?'

'It'll be M & S readies and some Merlot

that set me back four pounds thirty.'

'A wine of true distinction then. And don't they say it's the company that makes the meal?'

Out on the street, making towards his car in the clear light of an early spring evening, she said, 'Would *you* like me to move north?'

He glanced at her, thrown. 'What . . . can I say? I just want what is best for you. You deserve a life now, all you've been through. A decent bloke some day, maybe marriage and kids. If you think you might find it up here I wish you all the luck in the world.'

'I rather think I've given up on ordinary life, Frank, and men I can't connect with. Maybe one day, but a *lot* would need to change inside my head.'

They walked in silence, almost to where his car was parked, and then she said, 'You'd come and see me, wouldn't you? Surely you could give yourself a weekend off now and then.'

So far there'd not seemed a great deal of point to weekends off. His open-all-hours helped ease the pain of old wounds. He really didn't know what to say to her. What could the kid want with a man like him, apart from the fact that he knew what she'd gone through and the woman it had turned her into? She said she'd given up on normal life but it was what people were nearly always drawn back to in the end. Apart from him. 'Colette . . .'

'You need your funny way of life and I'm beginning to realize I need mine. But it can get lonely, yes, and it would be nice to have one good friend you can rely on. One who'd let me stay with him now and then and who'd come and stay with me. Absolutely no strings.' She looked up at him with a faint smile, the light catching her eyes in the setting sun. '*If* I came to live in Yorkshire.'

Crane watched her. She seemed to be saying she had his kind of baggage and had decided the only answer was to live the way he did, in society but not of it. But it wasn't easy and it helped if there was even one other outcast on the dark side of the palisade. As a way of life, for the sort of people events had made them into, it seemed difficult to improve on.

'That cottage you might be looking for: I could help you find it. I know the area, do you see.'

'Great!'

He opened the door of his Megane, paused. 'You drove up here. Where's your motor now?'

'Multi-storey, by the Norfolk Gardens.'

'Where are you staying tonight?'

'I'm sure I'll be able to get a room at the Norfolk. I can get a taxi from your place.' She began to grin. 'Unless you've got a better idea.'

Crane began to grin too. Began to feel better about himself than he'd felt for a very long time.

We do hope that you have enjoyed reading this large print book.

Did you know that all of our titles are available for purchase?

We publish a wide range of high quality large print books including:
Romances, Mysteries, Classics
General Fiction
Non Fiction and Westerns

Special interest titles available in large print are:
The Little Oxford Dictionary
Music Book
Song Book
Hymn Book
Service Book

Also available from us courtesy of Oxford University Press:
Young Readers' Dictionary
(large print edition)
Young Readers' Thesaurus
(large print edition)

For further information or a free brochure, please contact us at:
Ulverscroft Large Print Books Ltd.,
The Green, Bradgate Road, Anstey,
Leicester, LE7 7FU, England.
Tel: (00 44) **0116 236 4325**
Fax: (00 44) **0116 234 0205**

OLD BONES BURIED UNDER

June Drummond

A storm ravaging southern England causes the collapse of the rubbish tip at Abbotsfell in the Chilterns. John Thorneycroft, a forensic psychiatrist on holiday with Chief Detective Inspector Fergus Lowry, discovers in the landslip a human skull — and with it a plaster cast of a much earlier hominid skull, possibly man's immediate predecessor. Are these the remains of a murder victim, and how are they linked to the fossil cast? From the old bones buried an aeon ago and the lies and secrets of the recent past, Thorneycroft must establish the motive and method of a murderer.

E